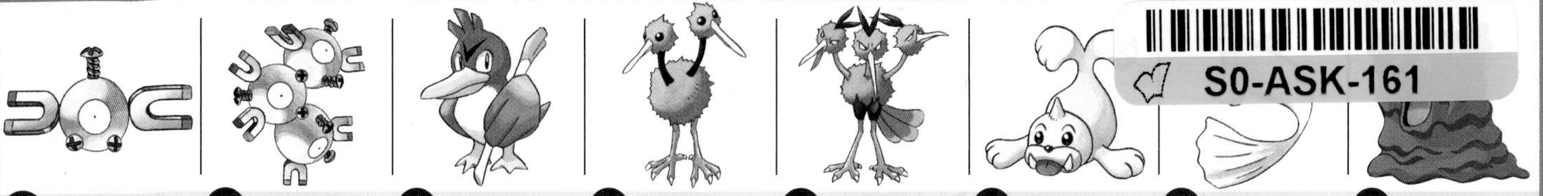

81 MAGNEMITE | 82 MAGNETON | 83 FARFETCH'D | 84 DODUO | 85 DODRIO | 86 SEEL | 87 DEWGONG | 88 GRIMER

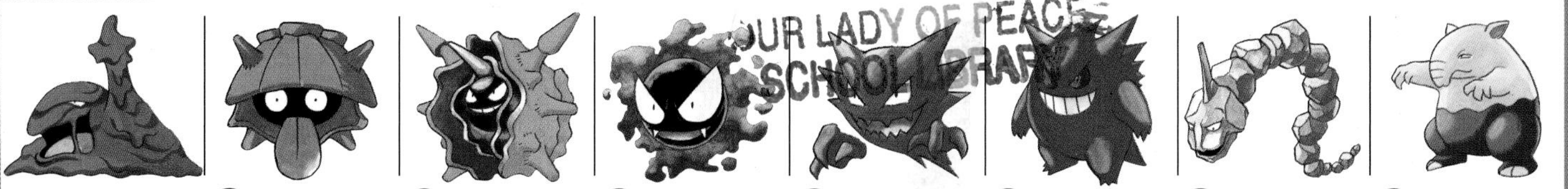

89 MUK | 90 SHELLDER | 91 CLOYSTER | 92 GASTLY | 93 HAUNTER | 94 GENGAR | 95 ONIX | 96 DROWZEE

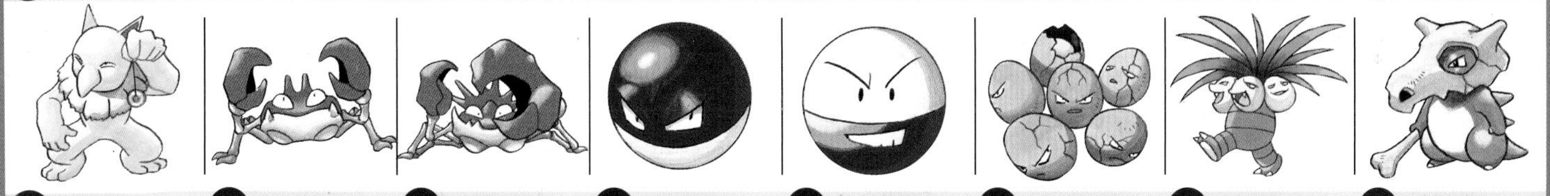

97 HYPNO | 98 KRABBY | 99 KINGLER | 100 VOLTORB | 101 ELECTRODE | 102 EXEGGCUTE | 103 EXEGGUTOR | 104 CUBONE

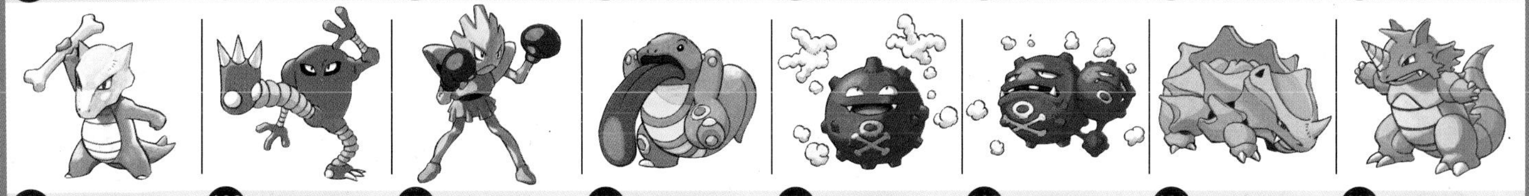

105 MAROWAK | 106 HITMONLEE | 107 HITMONCHAN | 108 LICKITUNG | 109 KOFFING | 110 WEEZING | 111 RHYHORN | 112 RHYDON

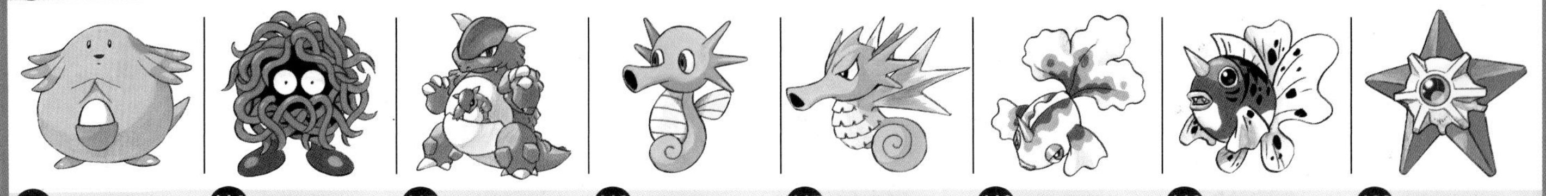

113 CHANSEY | 114 TANGELA | 115 KANGASKHAN | 116 HORSEA | 117 SEADRA | 118 GOLDEEN | 119 SEAKING | 120 STARYU

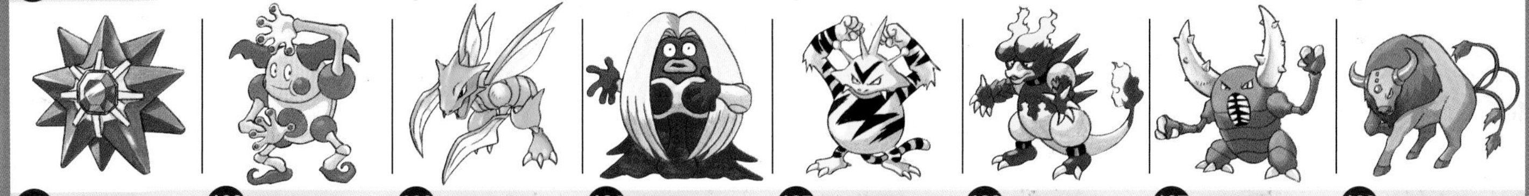

121 STARMIE | 122 MR.MIME | 123 SCYTHER | 124 JYNX | 125 ELECTABUZZ | 126 MAGMAR | 127 PINSIR | 128 TAUROS

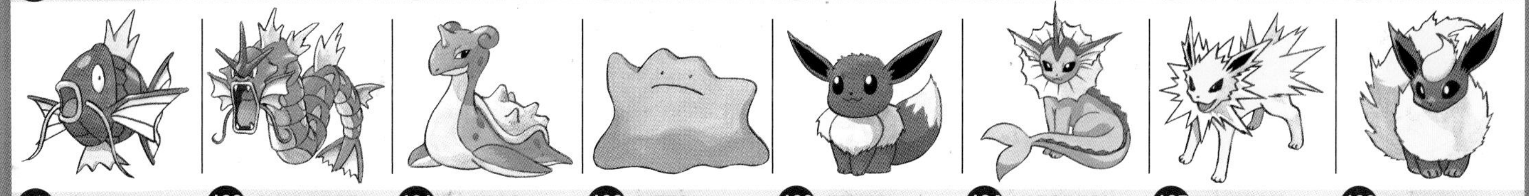

129 MAGIKARP | 130 GYARADOS | 131 LAPRAS | 132 DITTO | 133 EEVEE | 134 VAPOREON | 135 JOLTEON | 136 FLAREON

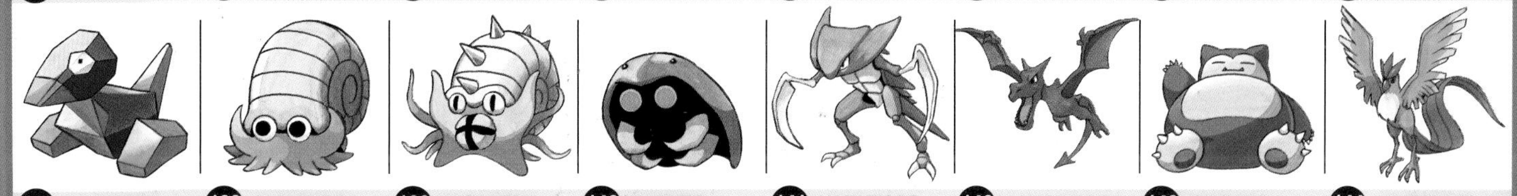

137 PORYGON | 138 OMANYTE | 139 OMASTAR | 140 KABUTO | 141 KABUTOPS | 142 AERODACTYL | 143 SNORLAX | 144 ARTICUNO

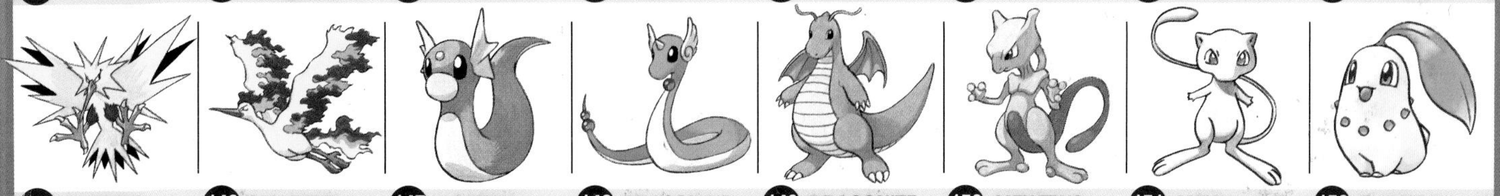

145 ZAPDOS | 146 MOLTRES | 147 DRATINI | 148 DRAGONAIR | 149 DRAGONITE | 150 MEWTWO | 151 MEW | 152 CHIKORITA

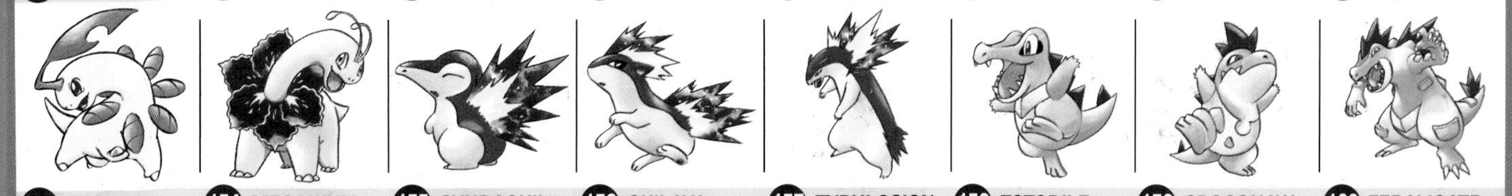

153 BAYLEEF | 154 MEGANIUM | 155 CYNDAQUIL | 156 QUILAVA | 157 TYPHLOSION | 158 TOTODILE | 159 CROCONAW | 160 FERALIGATR

Continued on page 28

LET'S FIND POKéMON!

TONS OF FUN AT THE AMUSEMENT PARK

How to have fun with this book:

1 Read the problems carefully and find the hidden Pokémon!

2 The answers are on page 24!

3 Also check out "Pokémon Problems" on page 25 and "Story Problems" on page 26!

4 Try doing the puzzles with your friends and family!

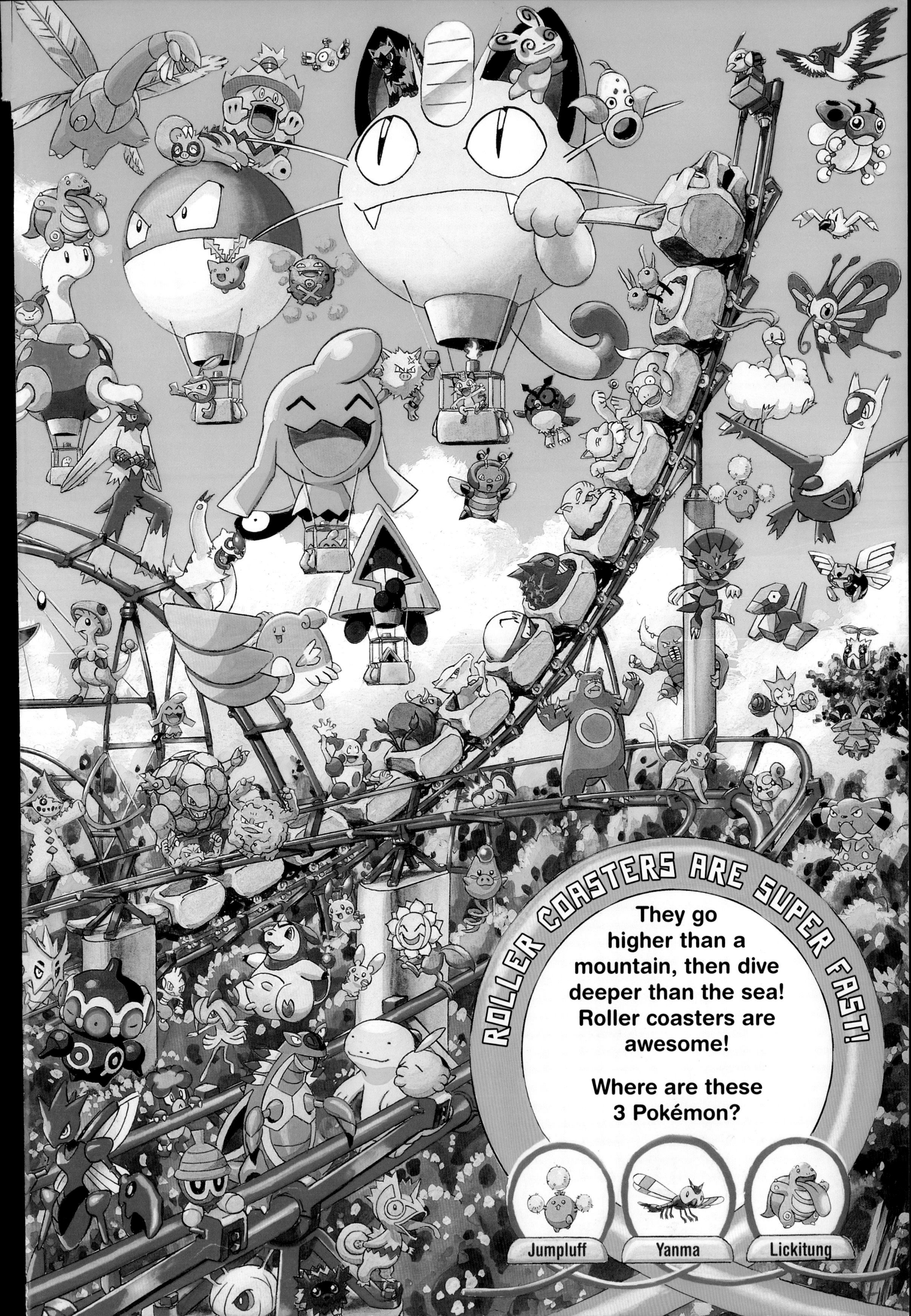
ROLLER COASTERS ARE SUPER FAST!
They go higher than a mountain, then dive deeper than the sea! Roller coasters are awesome!
Where are these 3 Pokémon?
Jumpluff
Yanma
Lickitung

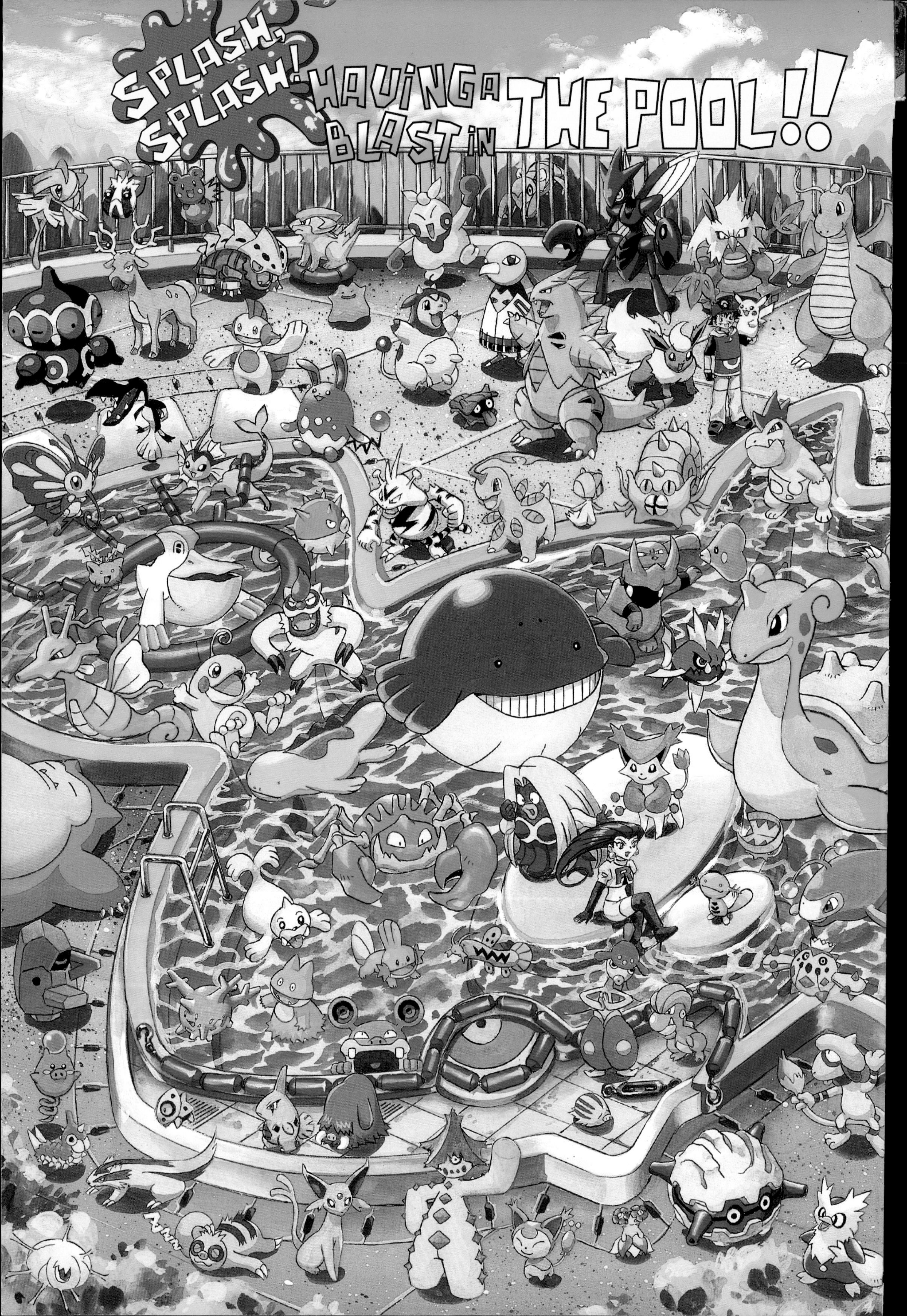
SPLASH, SPLASH!
HAVING A BLAST IN THE POOL!!

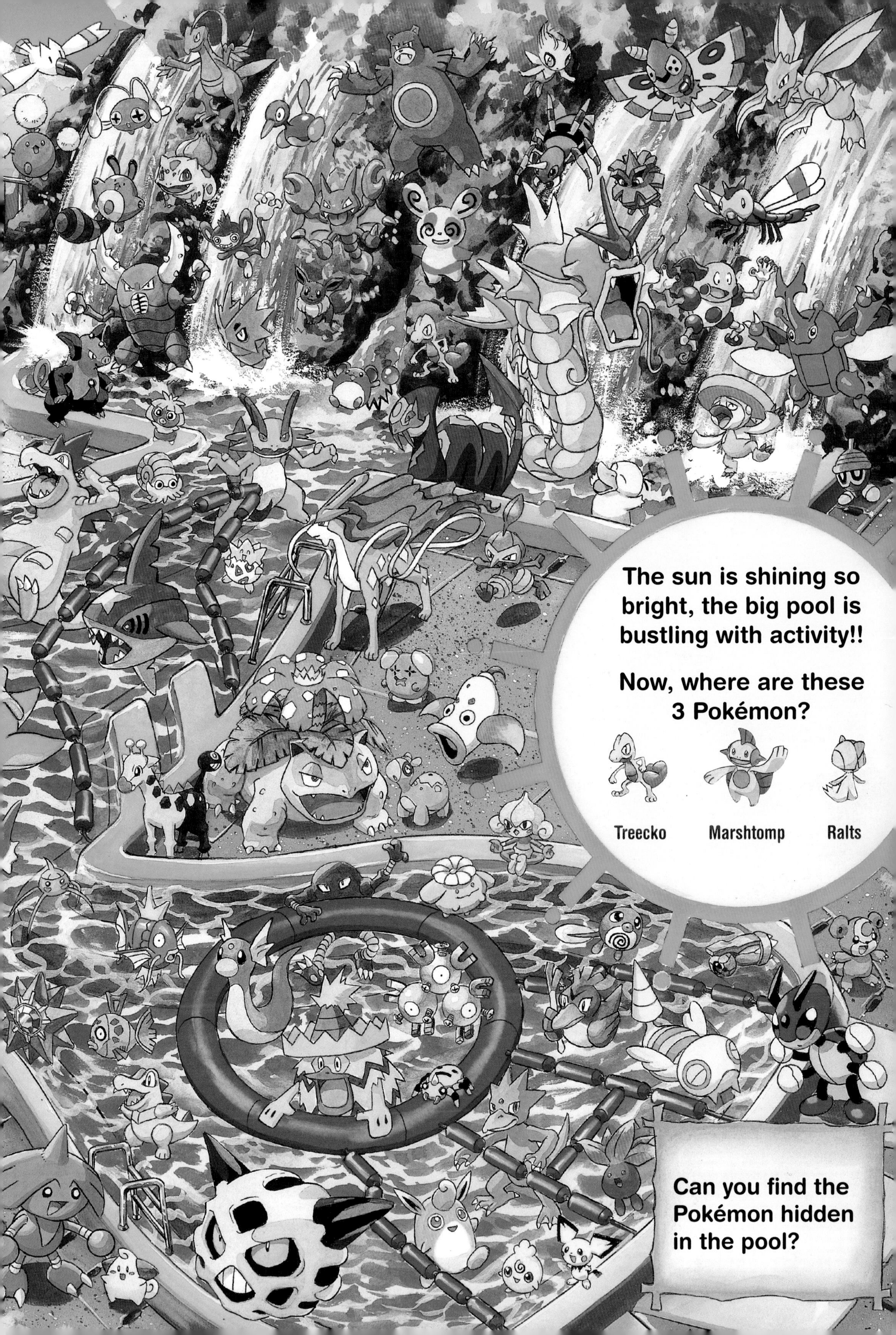
The sun is shining so bright, the big pool is bustling with activity!!
Now, where are these 3 Pokémon?
Treecko
Marshtomp
Ralts
Can you find the Pokémon hidden in the pool?

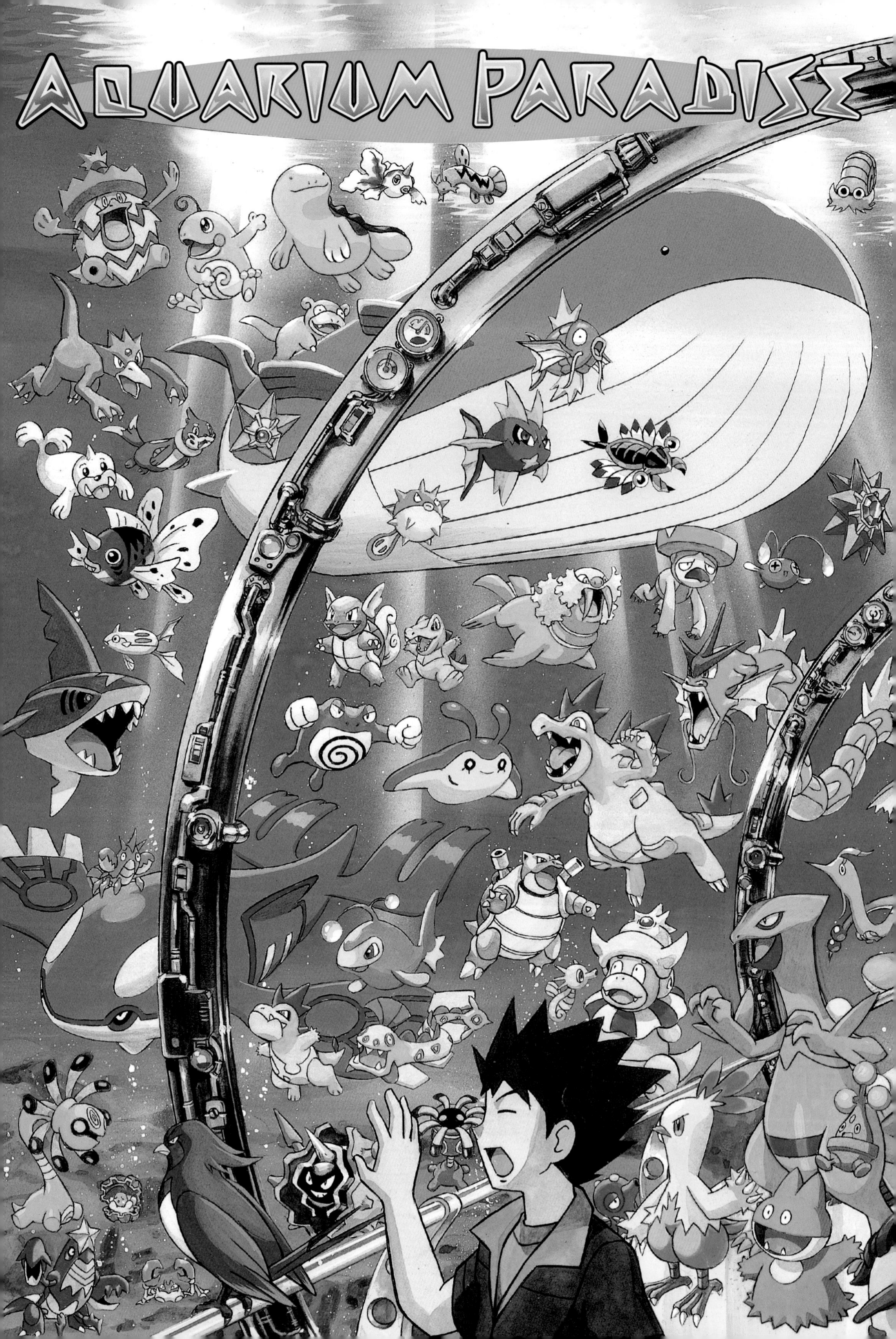
AQUARIUM PARADISE

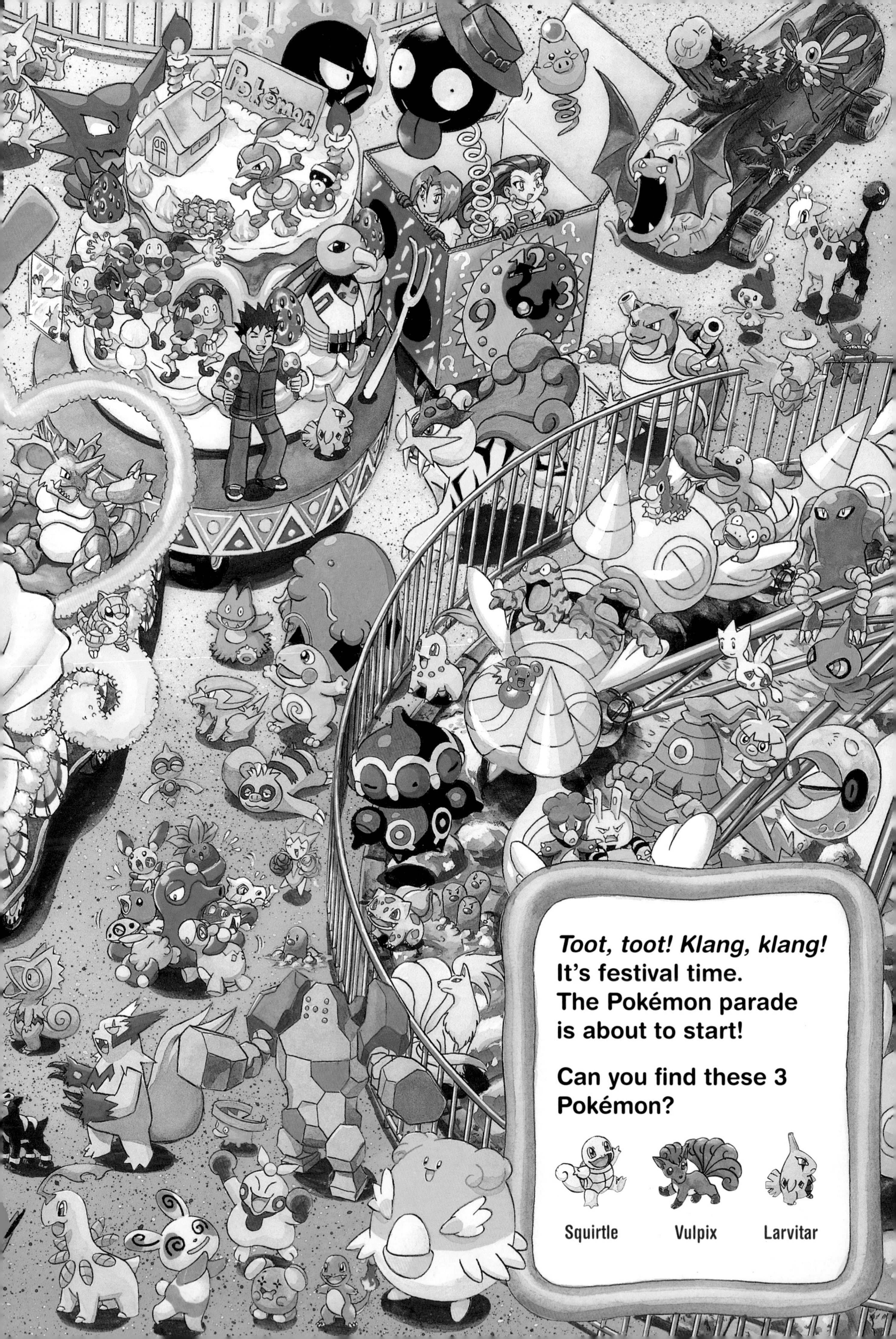
Pokémon

Toot, toot! Klang, klang!
It's festival time.
The Pokémon parade
is about to start!

Can you find these 3
Pokémon?

Squirtle Vulpix Larvitar

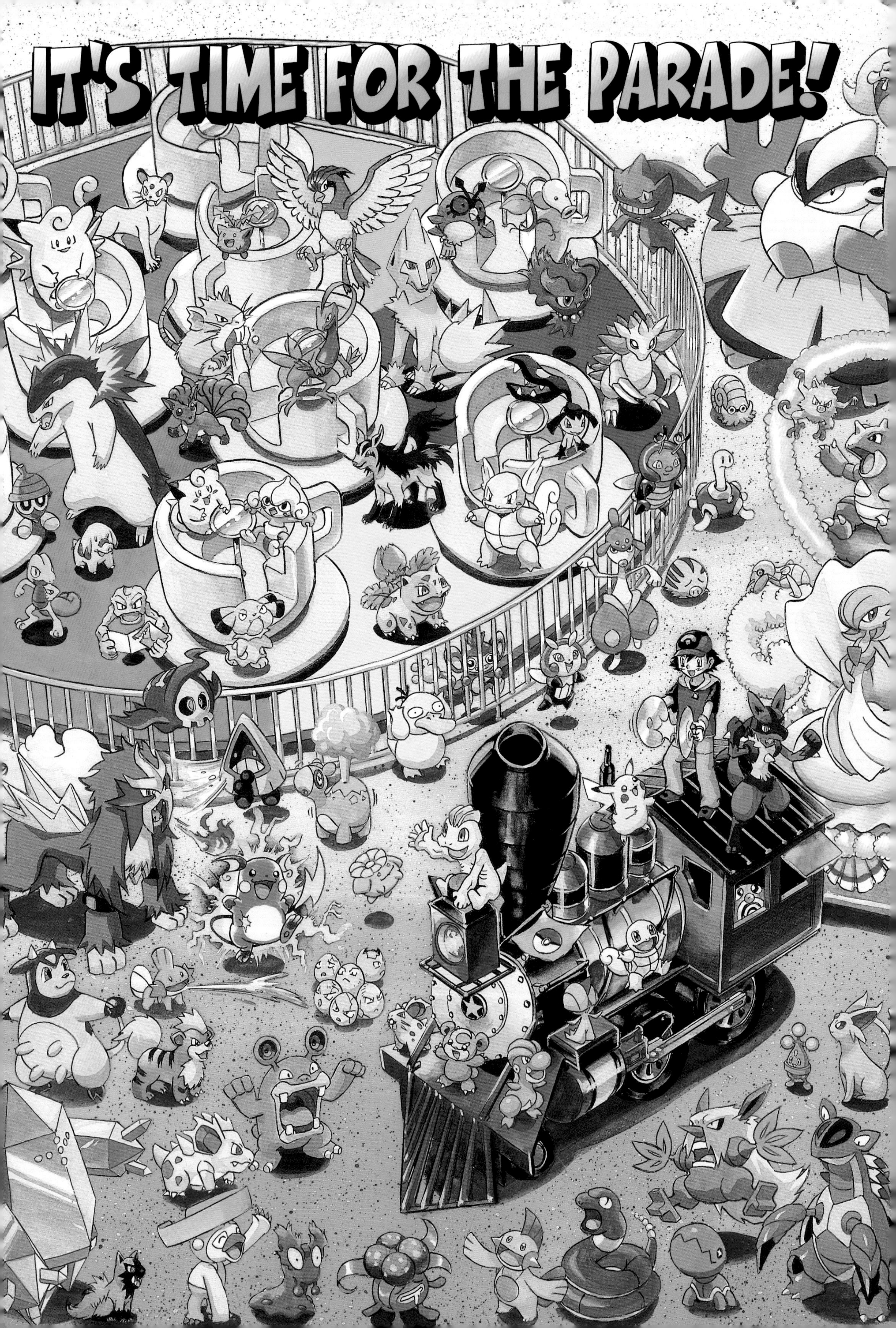
IT'S TIME FOR THE PARADE!

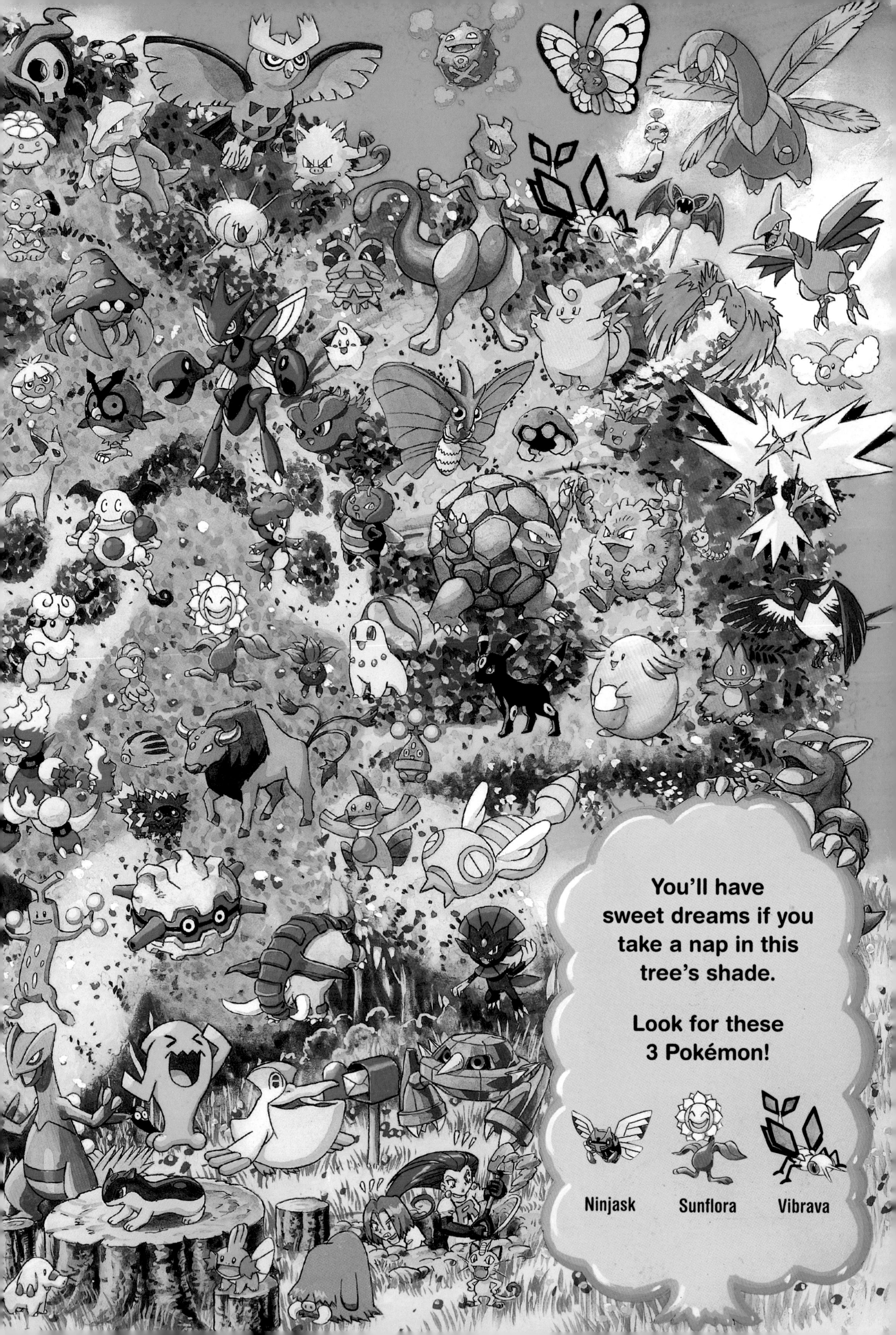
You'll have sweet dreams if you take a nap in this tree's shade.
Look for these 3 Pokémon!
Ninjask
Sunflora
Vibrava

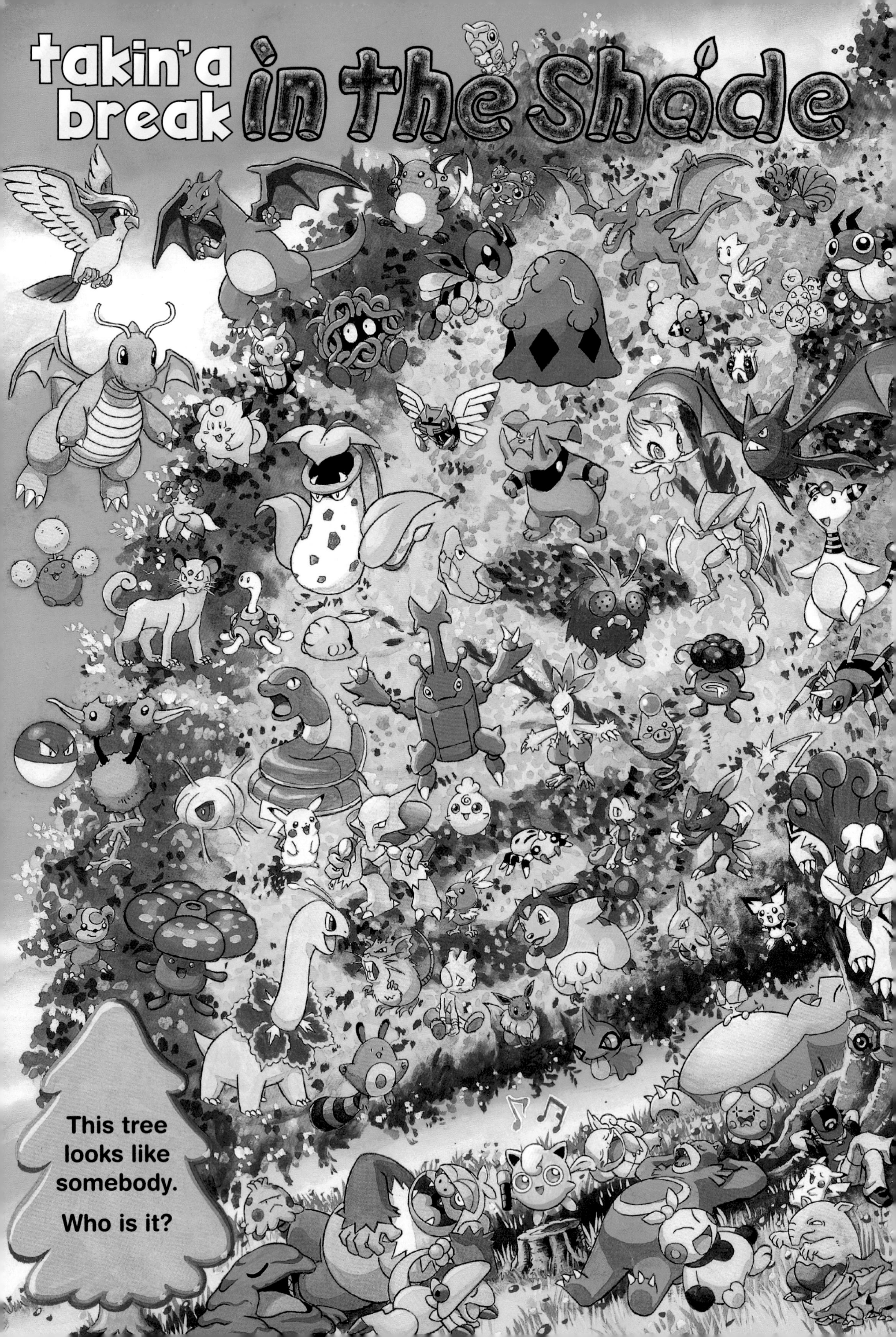
takin' a break in the Shade
This tree looks like somebody.
Who is it?

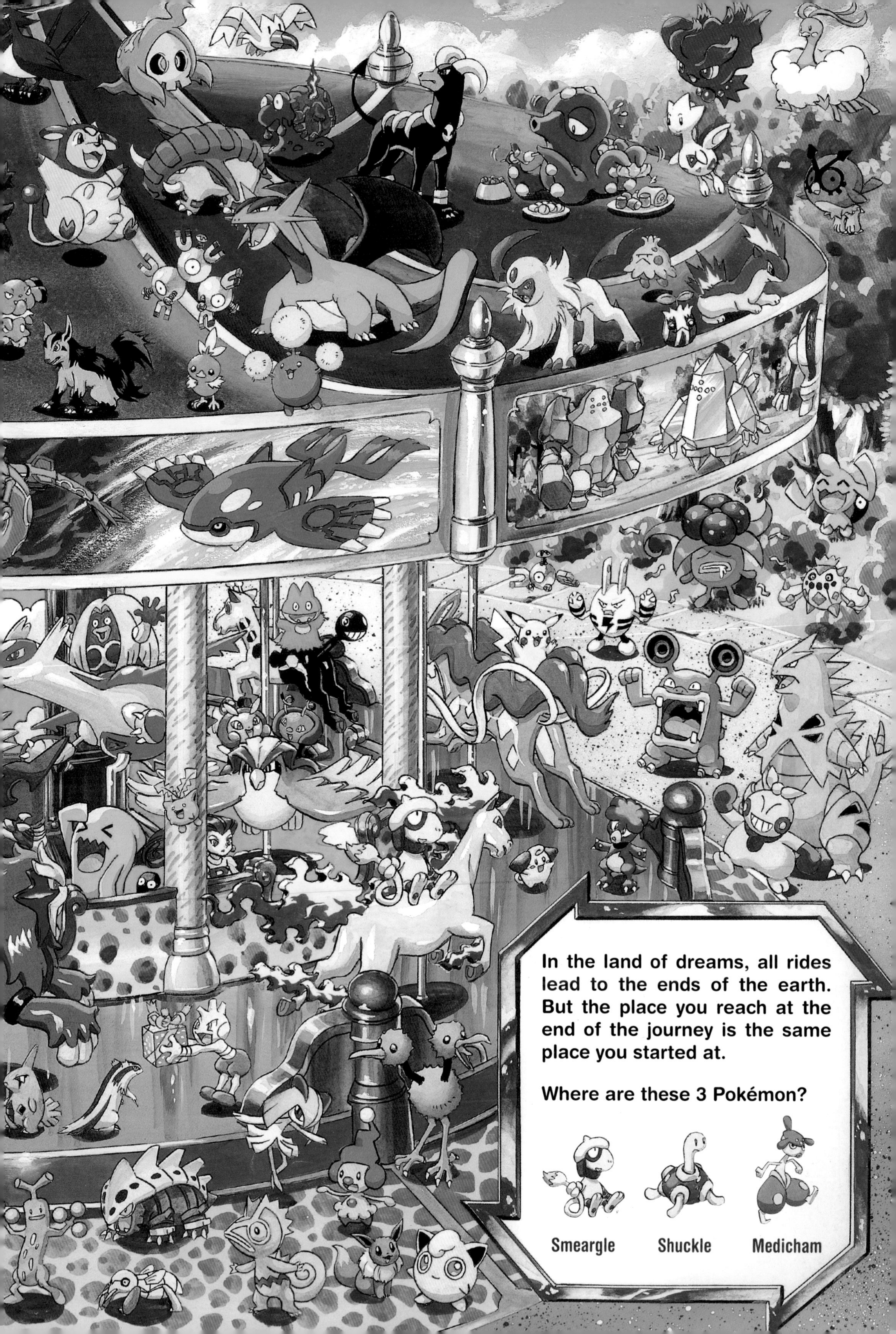
In the land of dreams, all rides lead to the ends of the earth. But the place you reach at the end of the journey is the same place you started at.
Where are these 3 Pokémon?
Smeargle
Shuckle
Medicham

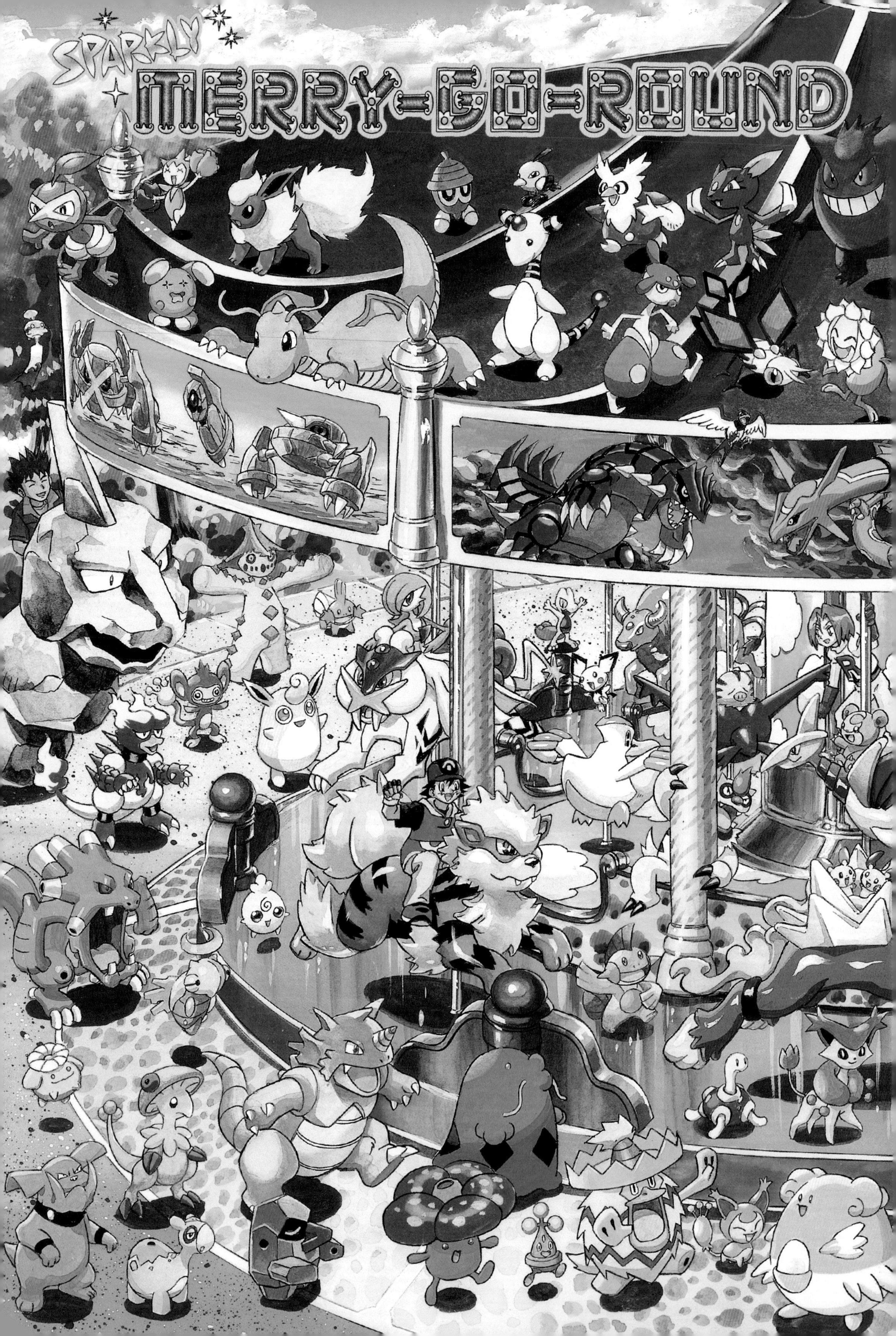
SPARKLY
MERRY-GO-ROUND

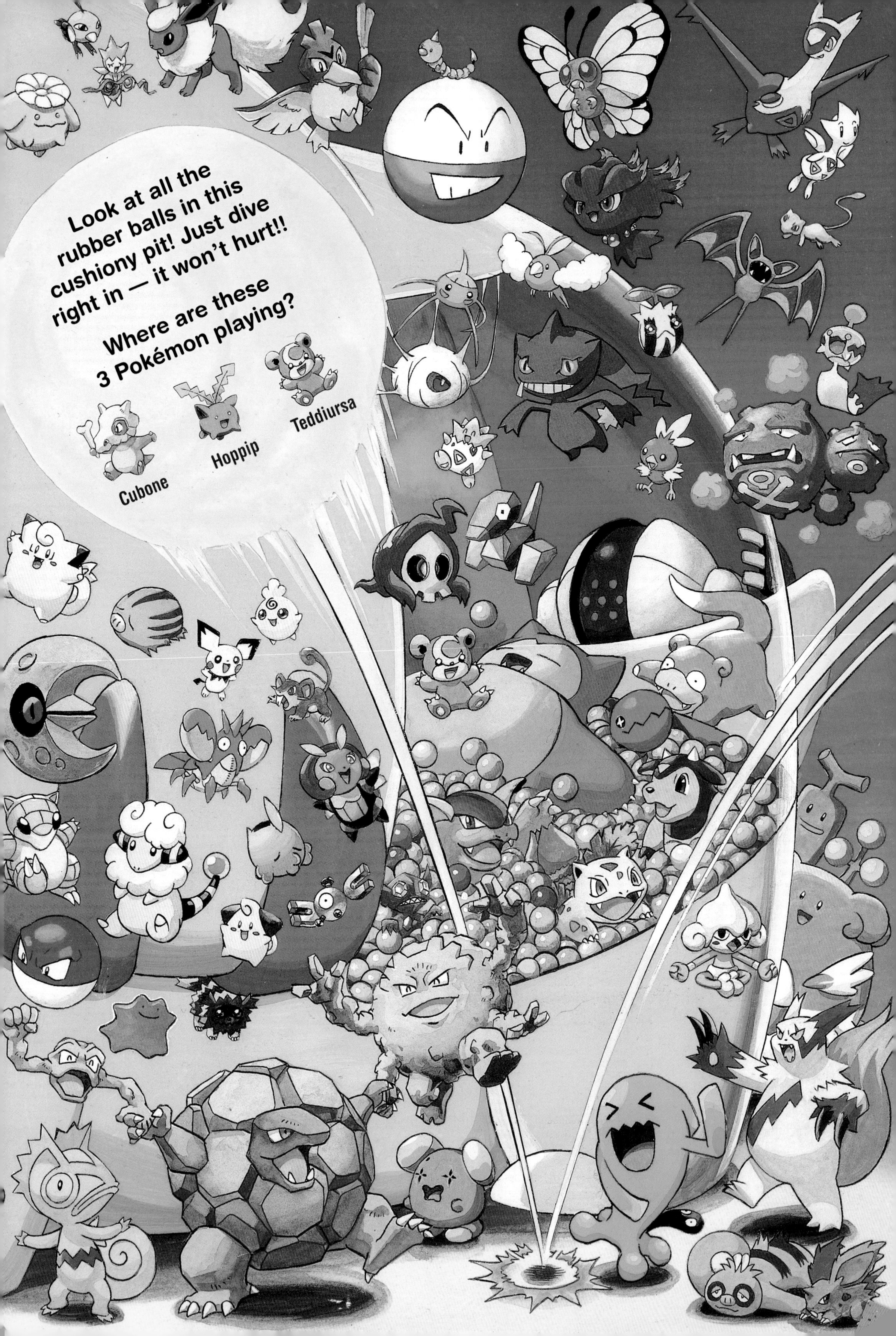
Look at all the rubber balls in this cushiony pit! Just dive right in — it won't hurt!!
Where are these 3 Pokémon playing?
Cubone
Hoppip
Teddiursa

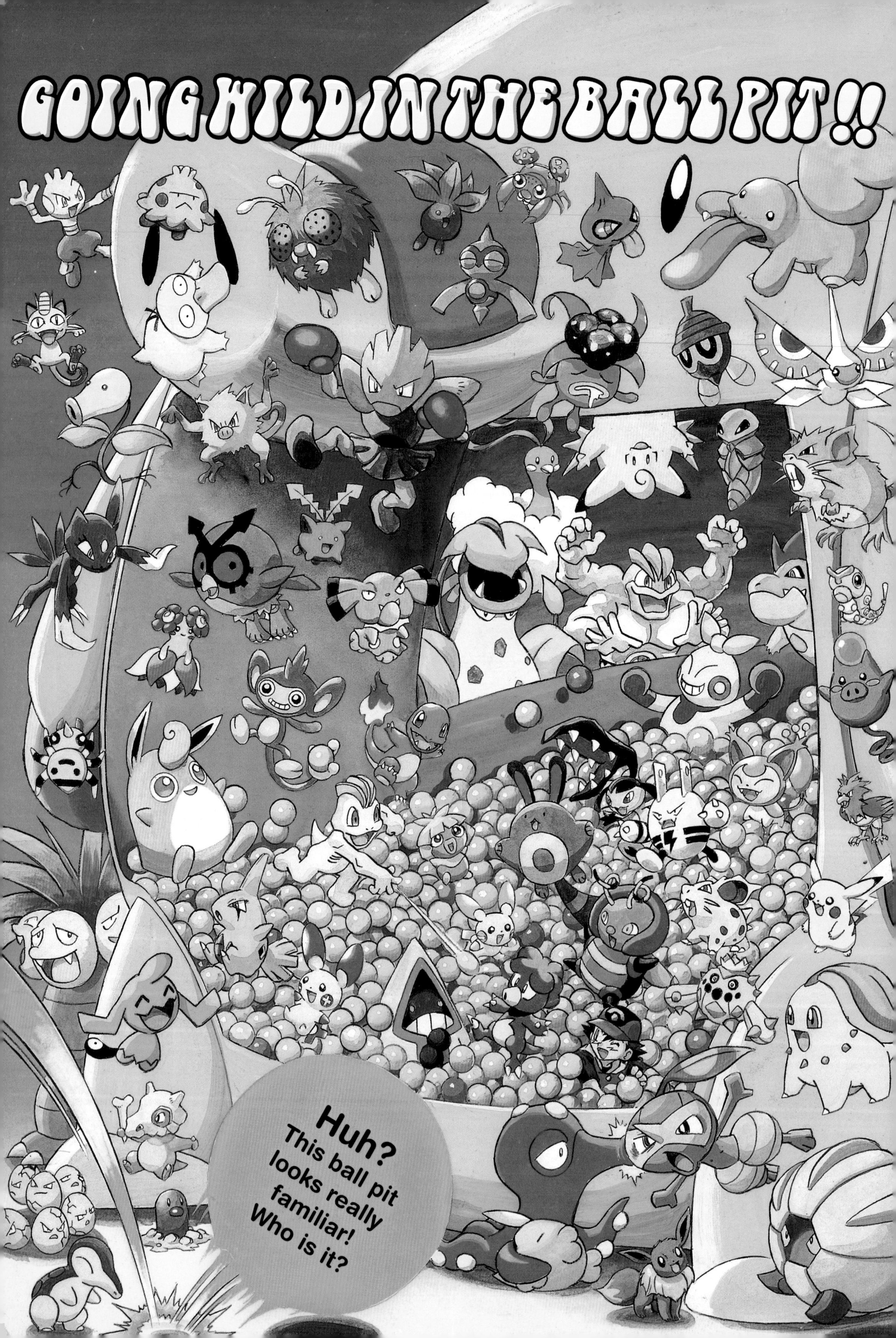
GOING WILD IN THE BALL PIT!!
Huh? This ball pit looks really familiar! Who is it?

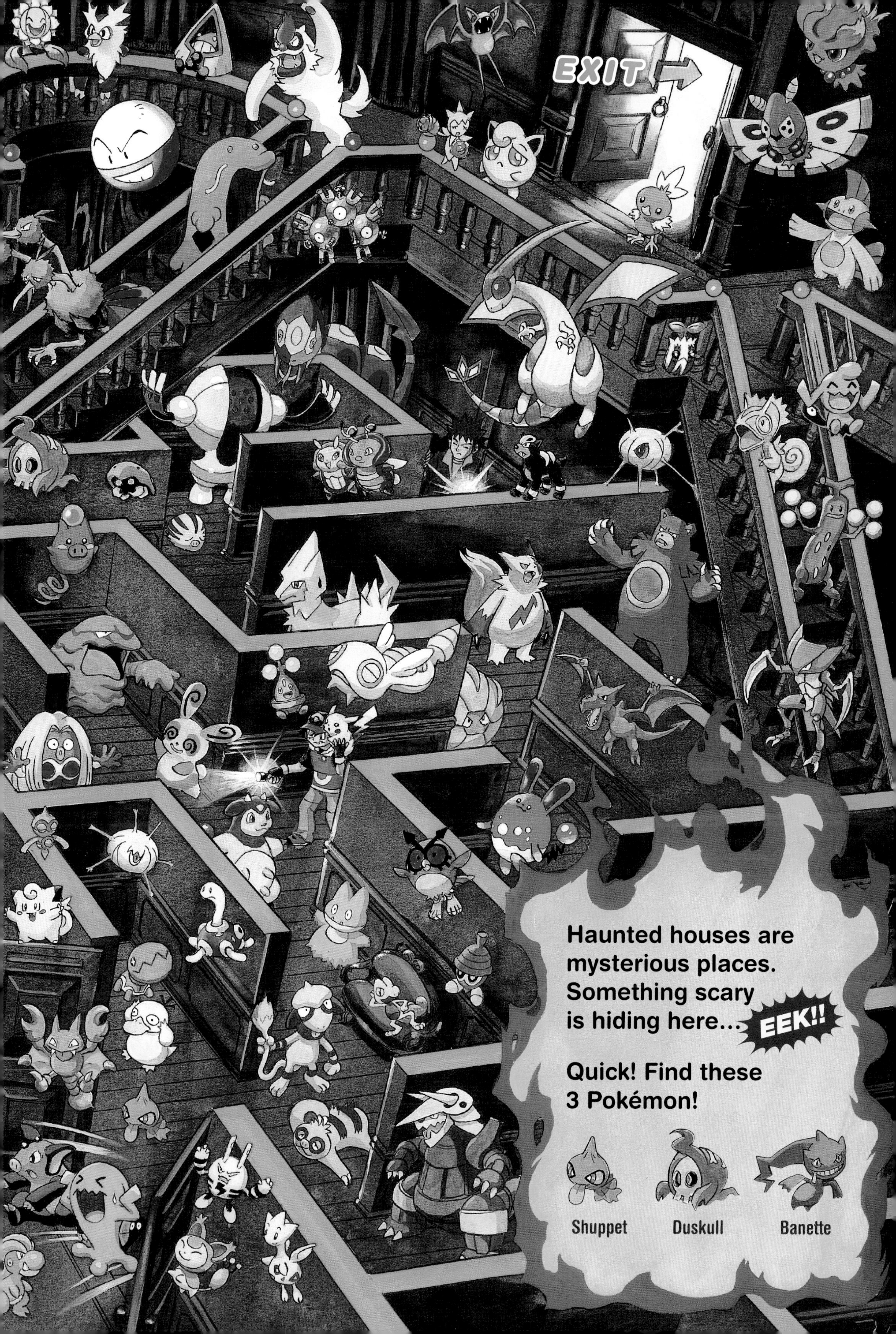
EXIT
Haunted houses are mysterious places. Something scary is hiding here...
EEK!!
Quick! Find these 3 Pokémon!
Shuppet
Duskull
Banette

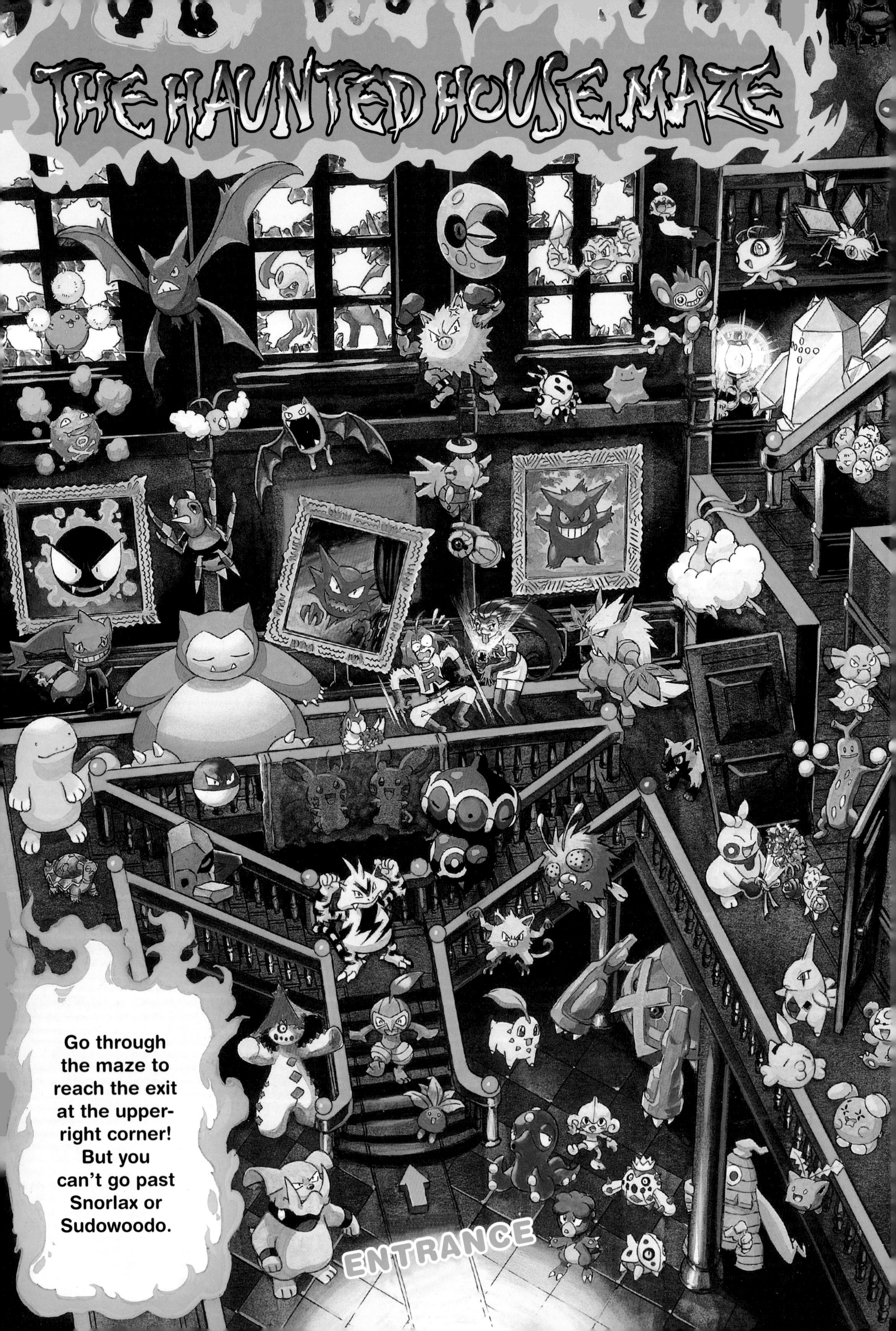
THE HAUNTED HOUSE MAZE
Go through the maze to reach the exit at the upper-right corner! But you can't go past Snorlax or Sudowoodo.
ENTRANCE

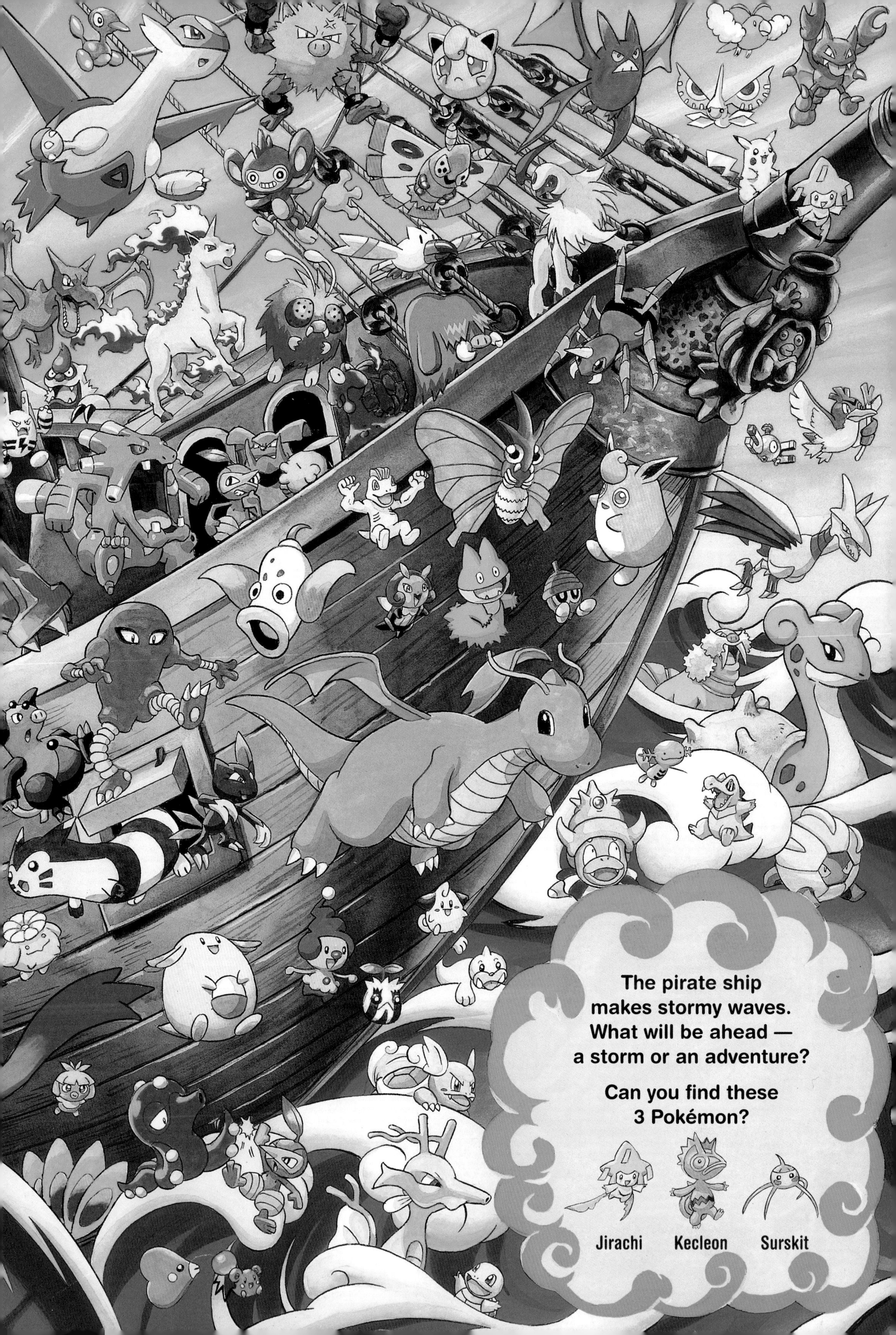
The pirate ship
makes stormy waves.
What will be ahead —
a storm or an adventure?
Can you find these
3 Pokémon?
Jirachi
Kecleon
Surskit

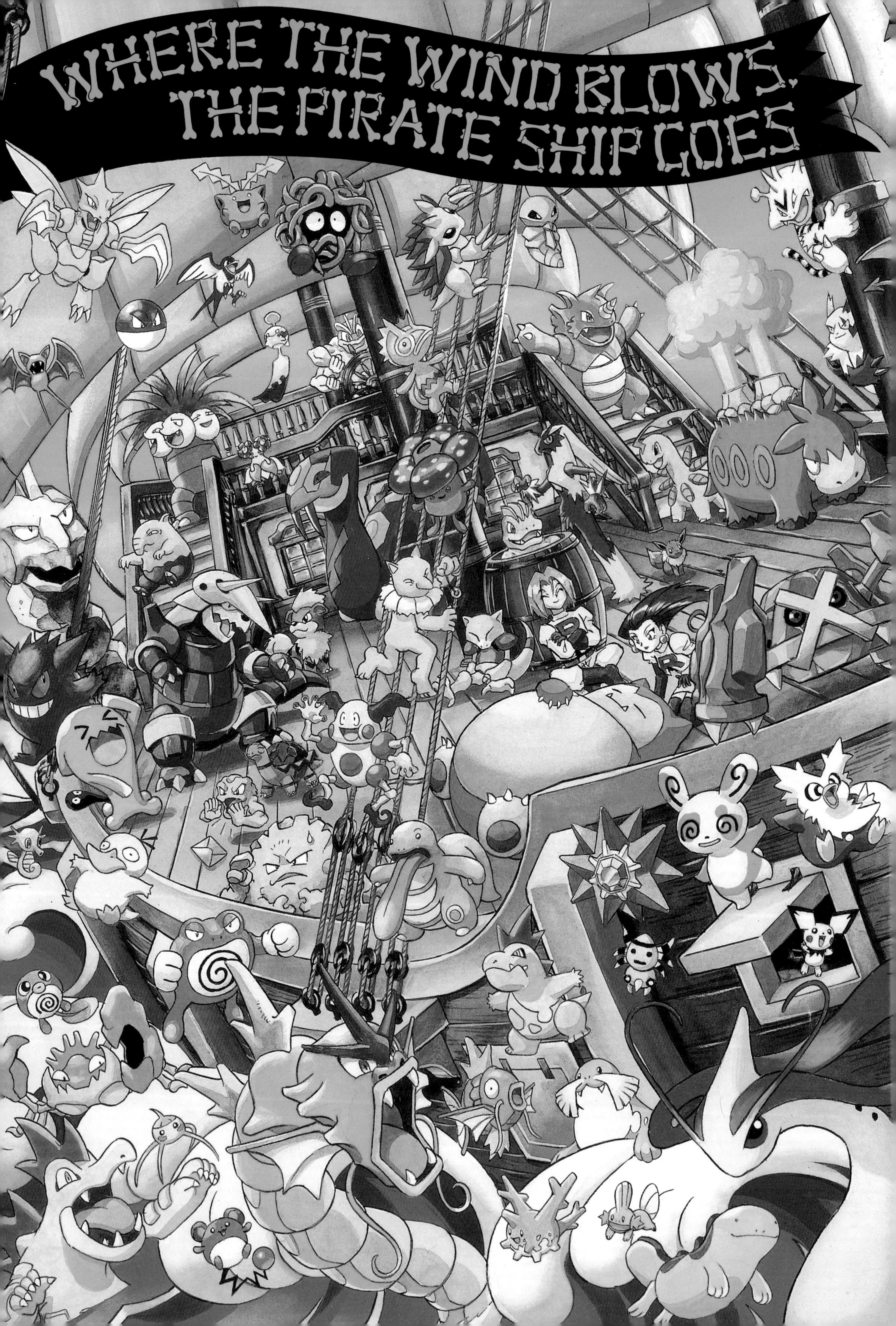
WHERE THE WIND BLOWS,
THE PIRATE SHIP GOES

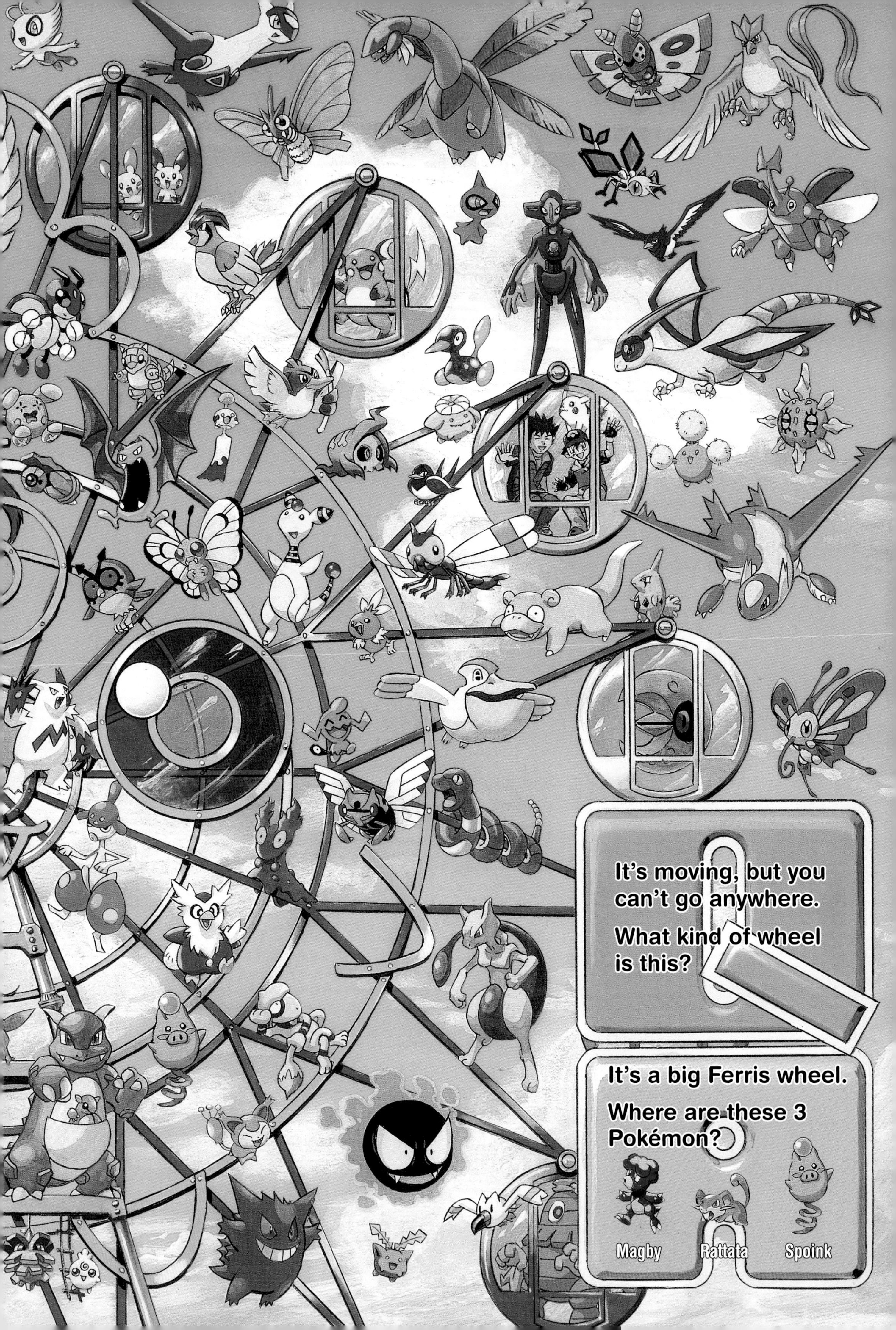
It's moving, but you can't go anywhere.
What kind of wheel is this?
It's a big Ferris wheel.
Where are these 3 Pokémon?
Magby
Rattata
Spoink

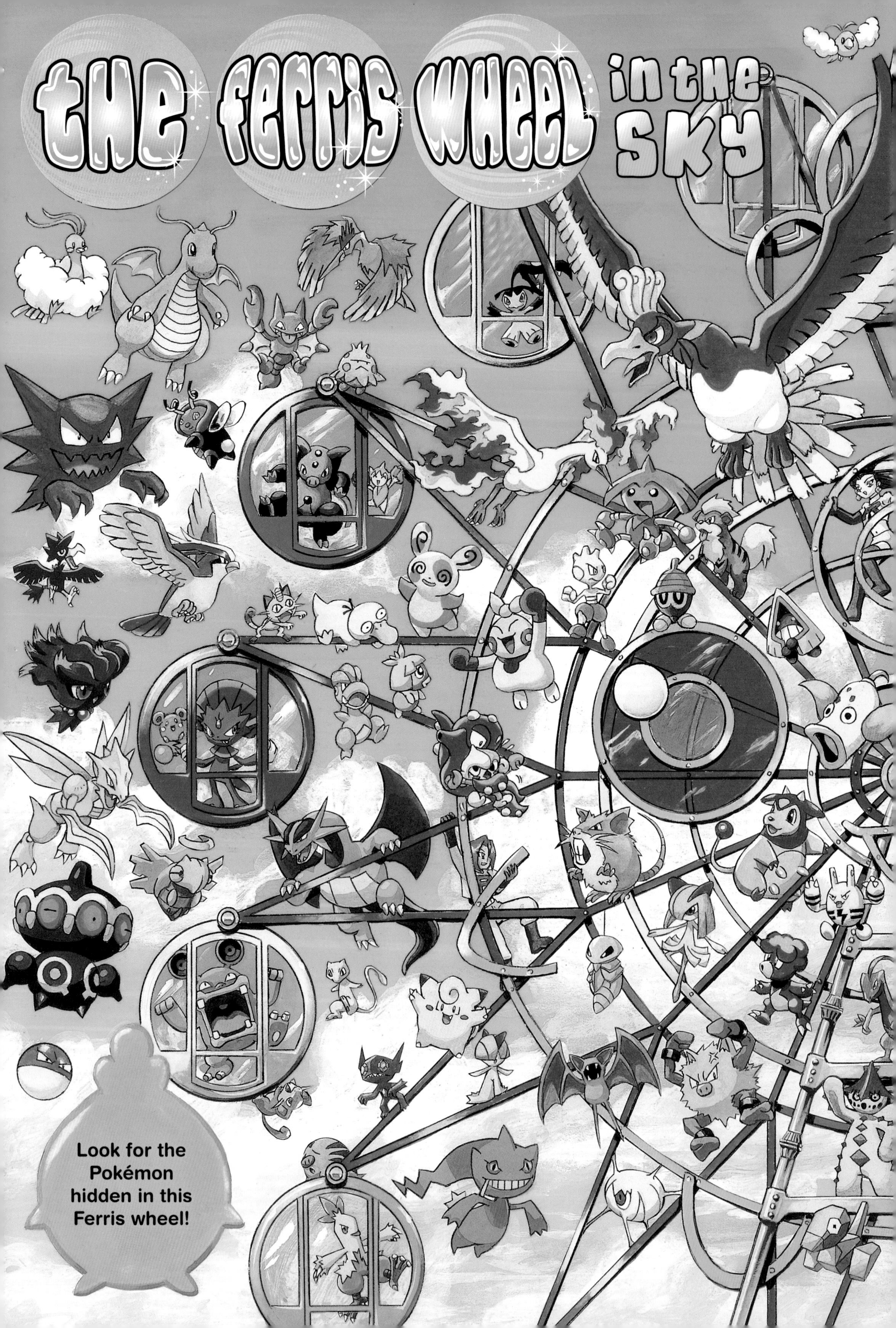
The Ferris Wheel in the Sky
Look for the Pokémon hidden in this Ferris wheel!

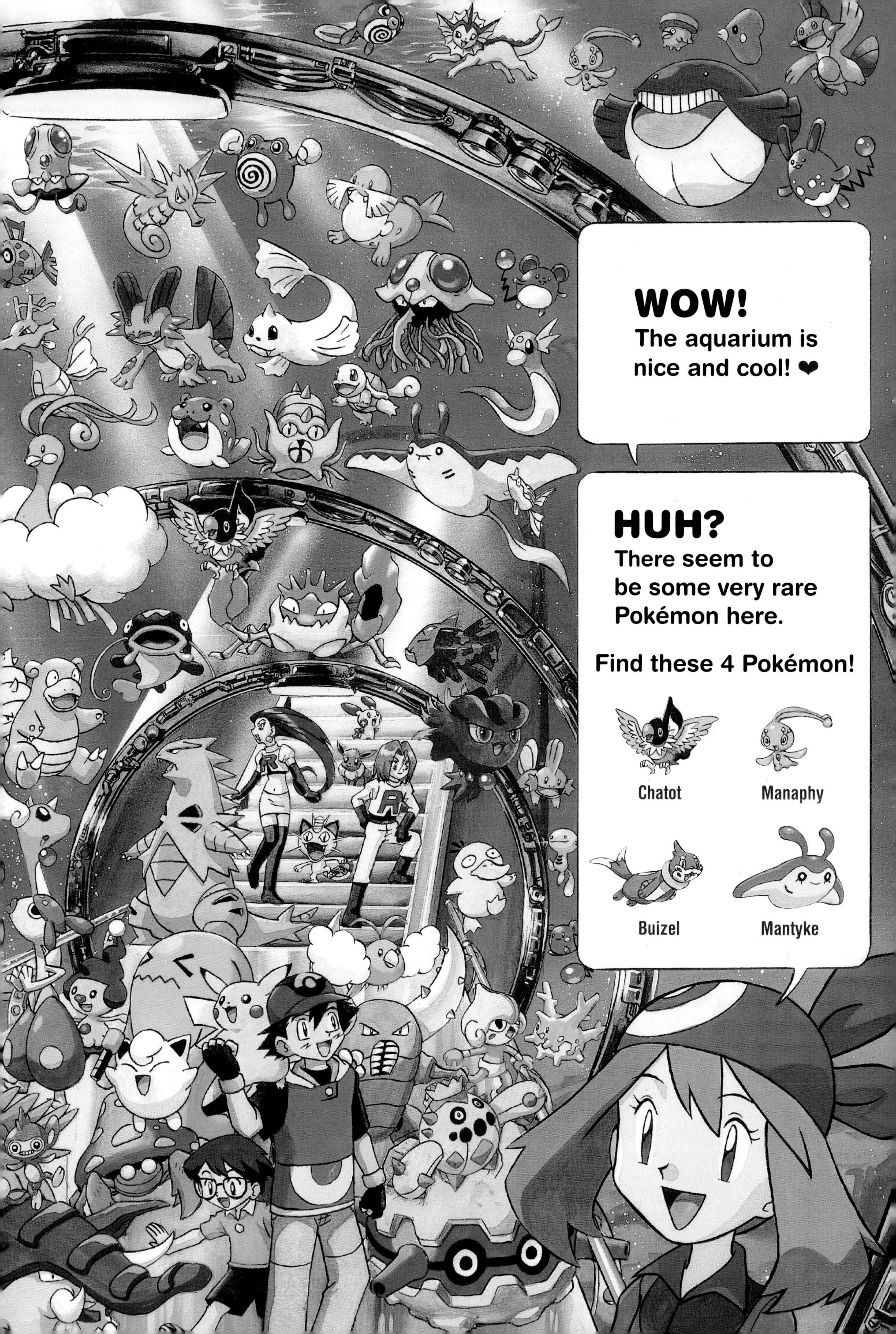
WOW!
The aquarium is nice and cool! ❤
HUH?
There seem to be some very rare Pokémon here.
Find these 4 Pokémon!
Chatot
Manaphy
Buizel
Mantyke

The ANSWERS!

Turn the book sideways to view this page!

Which Pokémon is hidden in this page? (The answer is on page 31.)

● Roller Coasters Are Super Fast!

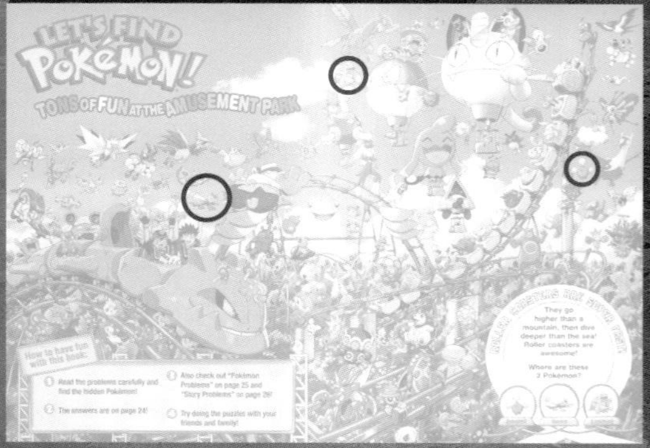
LET'S FIND POKéMON!
TONS OF FUN AT THE AMUSEMENT PARK

● Splash, Splash! Having a Blast in the Pool!!

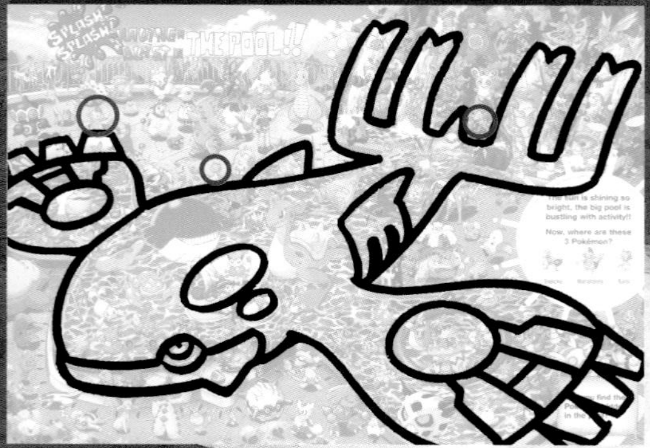

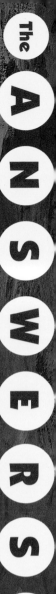

KYOGRE is the Pokémon that's hiding.

● The Ferris Wheel in the Sky

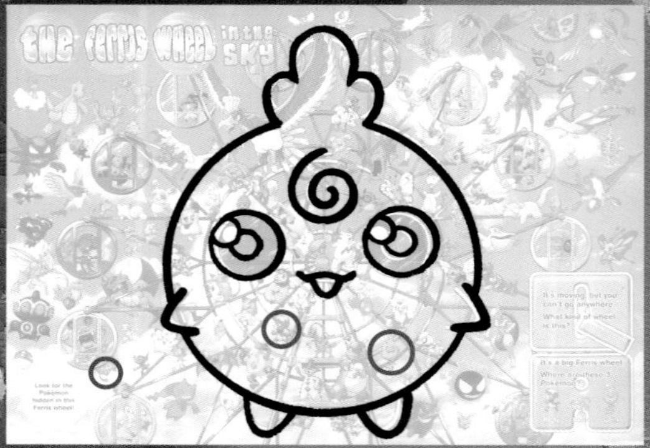

IGGLYBUFF is the Pokémon that's hiding.

● Where the Wind Blows, the Pirate Ship Goes

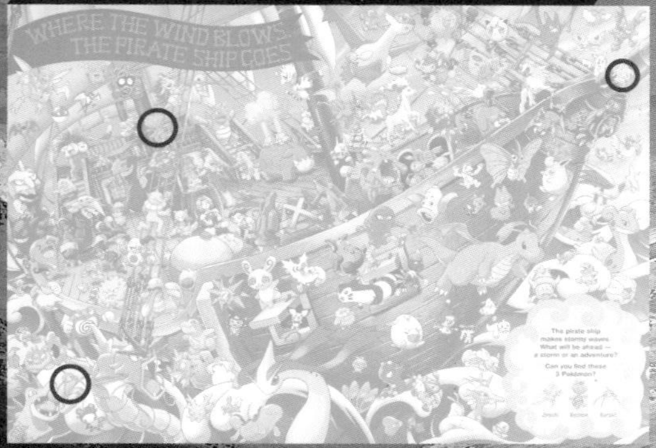

● The Haunted House Maze

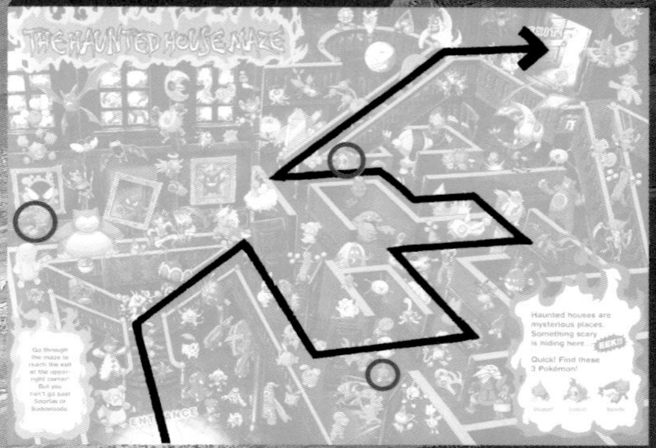

● Going Wild in the Ball Pit!!

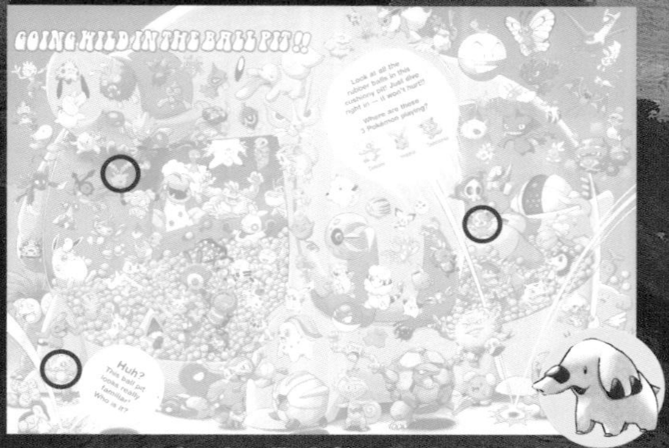

PHANPY is the Pokémon that's hiding.

● Sparkly Merry-Go-Round

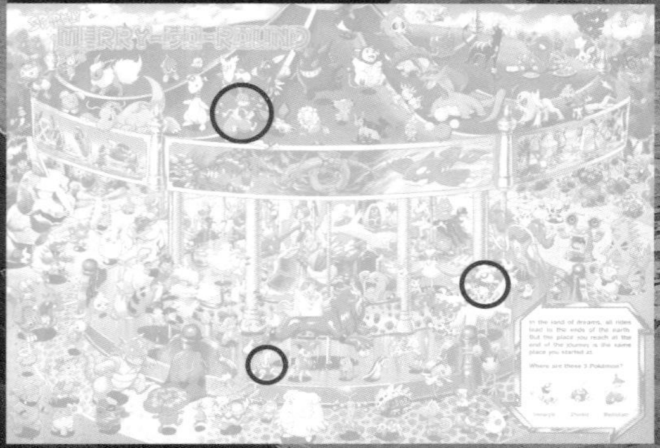

● Takin' a Break in the Shade

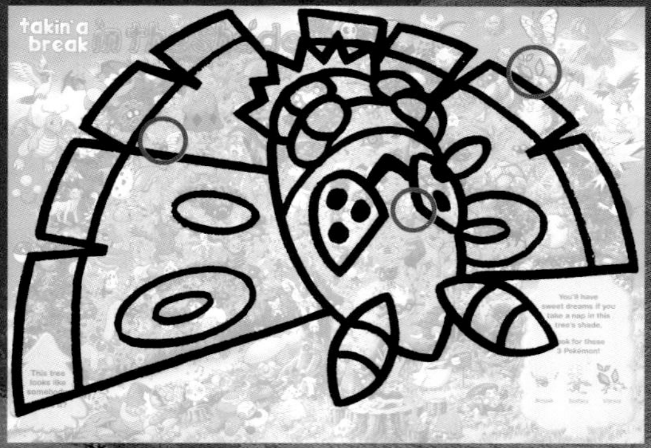

● It's Time for the Parade!

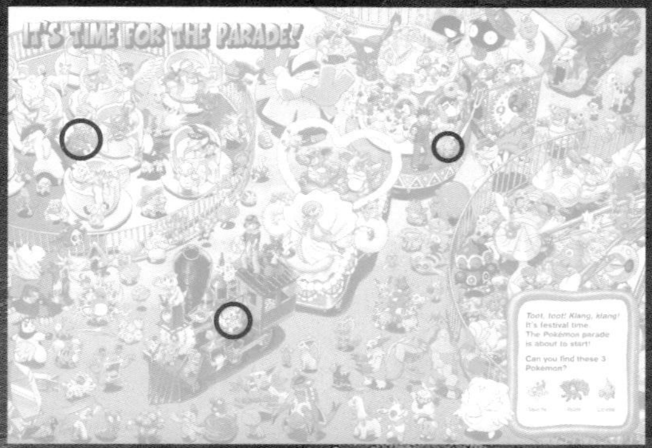
IT'S TIME FOR THE PARADE!

● Aquarium Paradise

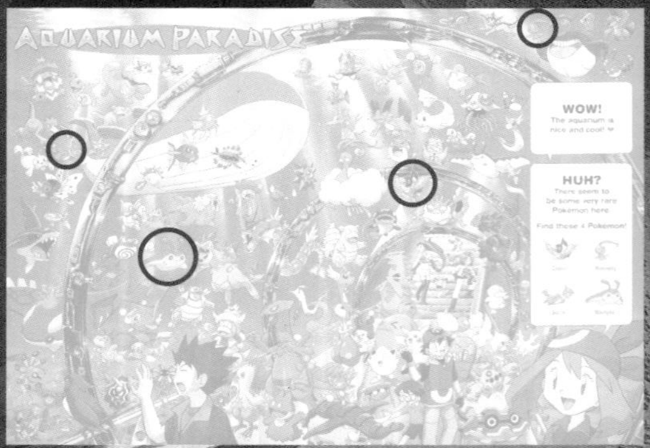
WOW!
HUH?

If you turn it upside down, you'll find **DUSTOX**.

Pokémon Problems

The tip of its tail shines with light! Where is this Ampharos?

It smells like honey to lure prey into its mouth.

Where is this Goldeen, nicknamed the Water Queen?

Ampharos

Victreebel

Goldeen

It can float in the sky without even moving its wings. Where is this Togetic?

It's incredibly stinky. You can smell it over a mile away!

It sleeps 20 hours a day! Where is it sleeping?

Gloom

Slakoth

The thorns on its head have a dangerous poison.

Its weakness is the rain. If it becomes wet, it can't fly.

It can purify dirty water in an instant.

Masquerain

Suicune

Look for them throughout the whole book.

(The answers are on page 31.)

Story Problem #1

The Invitation that Flies Through the Sky

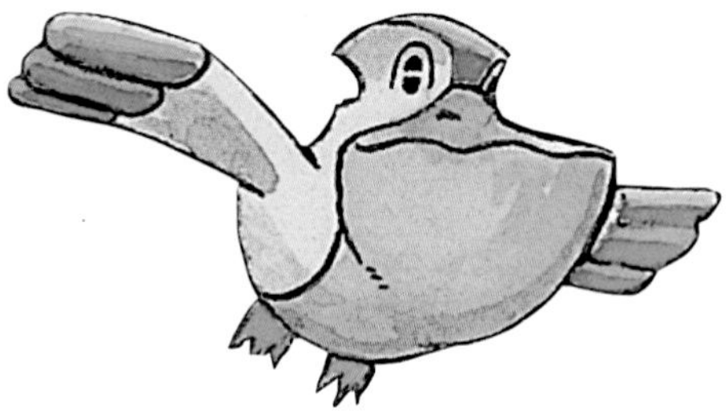

1 Pelipper is flying. Where is it going?

2 It's someone's mailbox — Pelipper was delivering a letter!

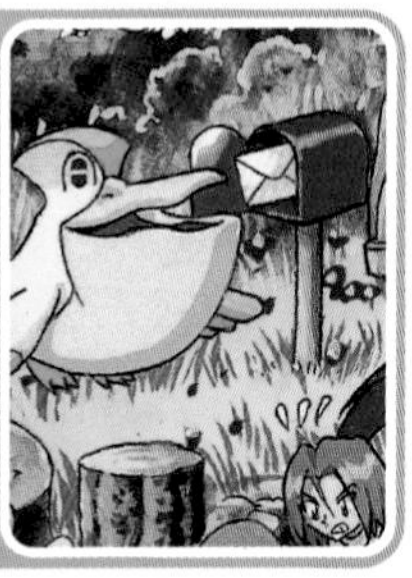

3 "Geodude! A letter came."

Geodude grabbed it.

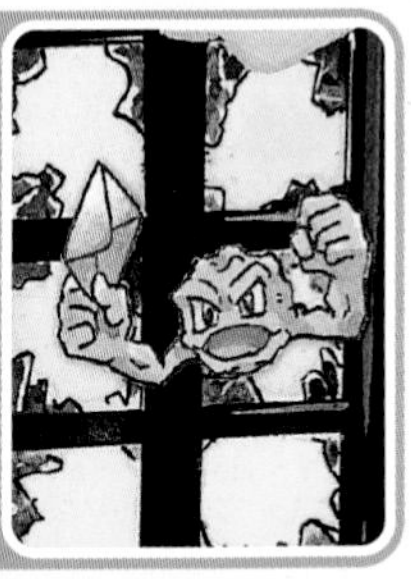

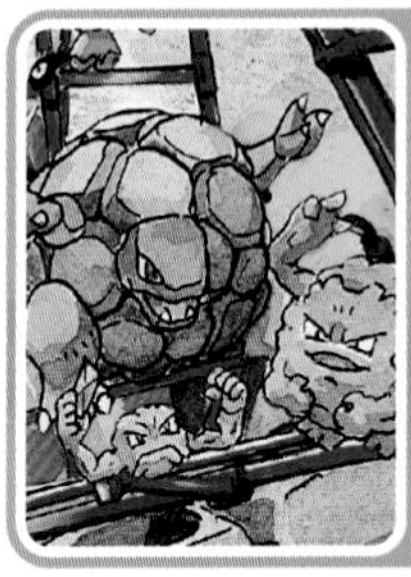

4 Graveler and Golem have also come.

"Can you read the letter out loud?"

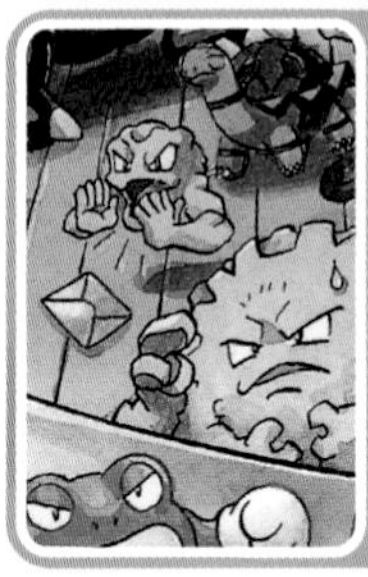

5 "Hey, Letter! Mr. Letter!!"

No, don't call it, read it.

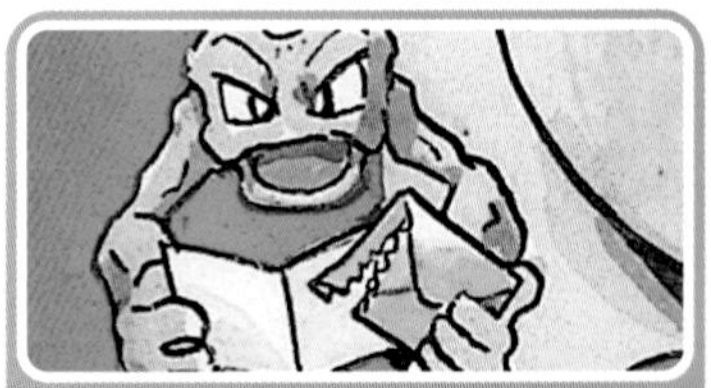

6 It says, "Everybody, please come to my birthday party! ❤"

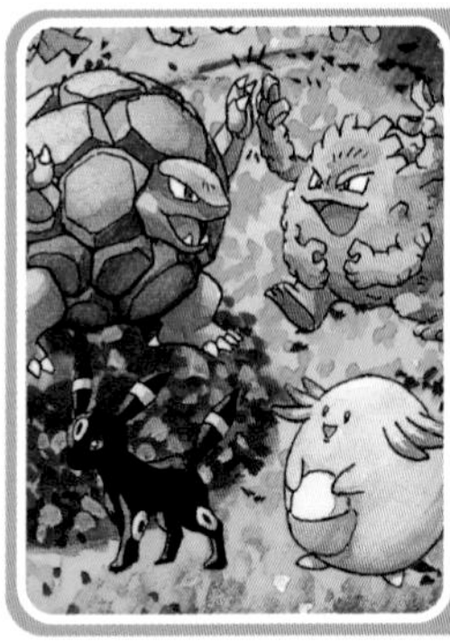

7 "Yay! A birthday party!"

"OK! Happy, lucky, Umbreon! ❤"

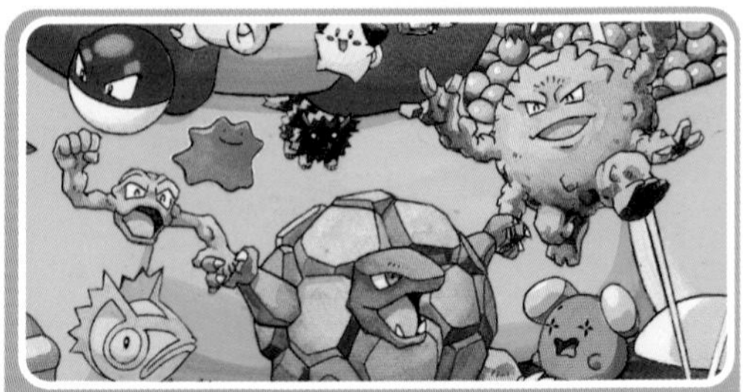

8 Everybody starts to dance with joy, but the party hasn't even started yet!

Story Problem #2

Is Octillery a Witch?!

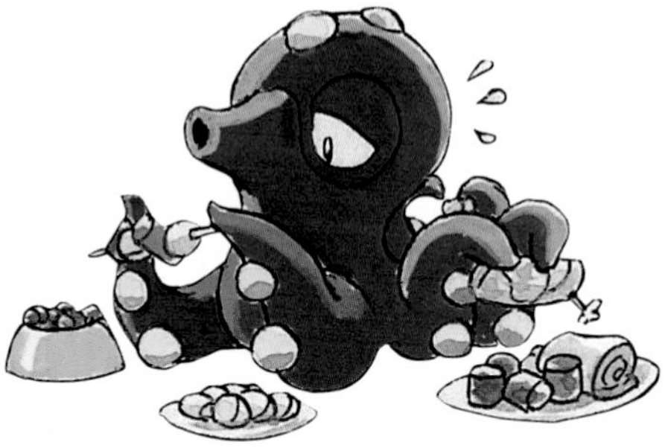

1 Octillery is making a feast for the party, using its many arms.

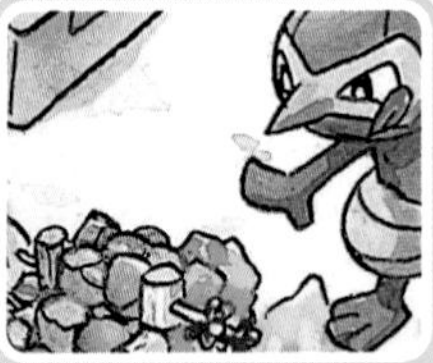

2 Let me just get a taste...

3 "No! You have to wait until the party starts!"

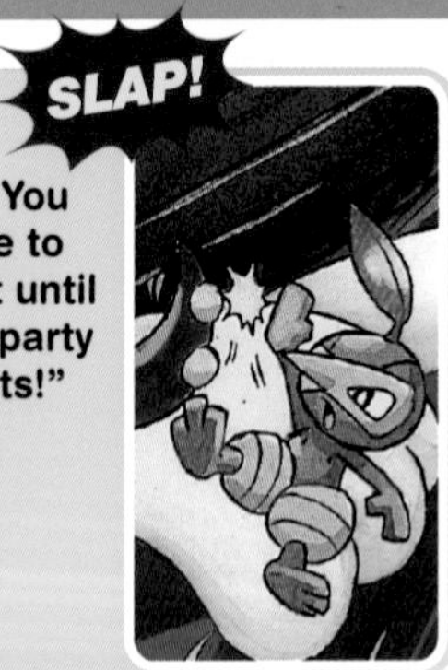
SLAP!

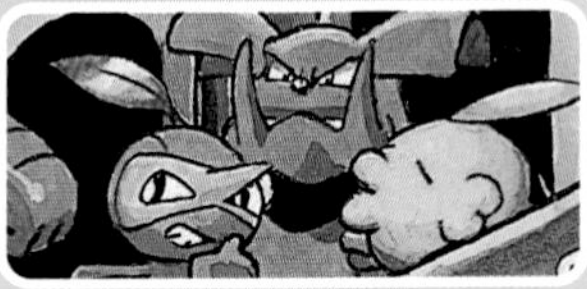

4 That makes me want to eat it even more.

Whisper, whisper. Sneak, sneak.

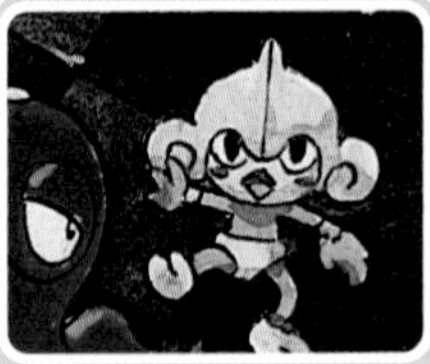

5 Hey Octillery, what a nice day it is today.

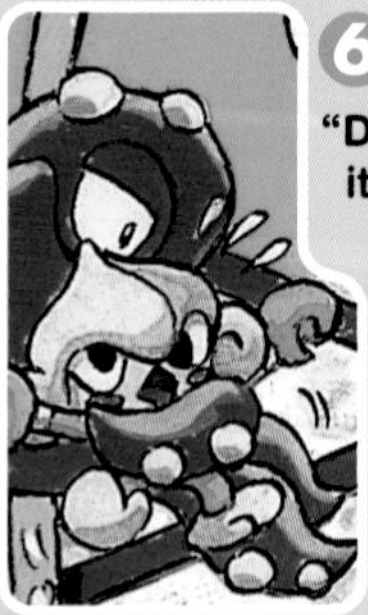

6 "Don't eat it yet!"

Octillery clings on frantically.

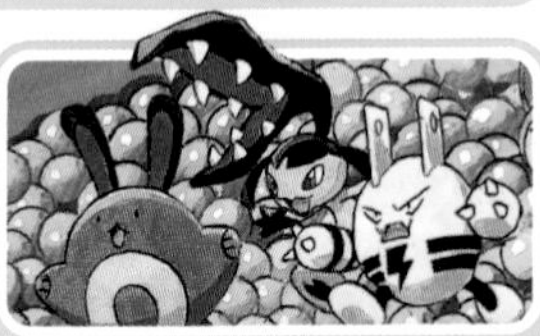

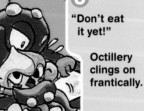

7 "We want to eat the food too!"

Everyone swarms in at once.

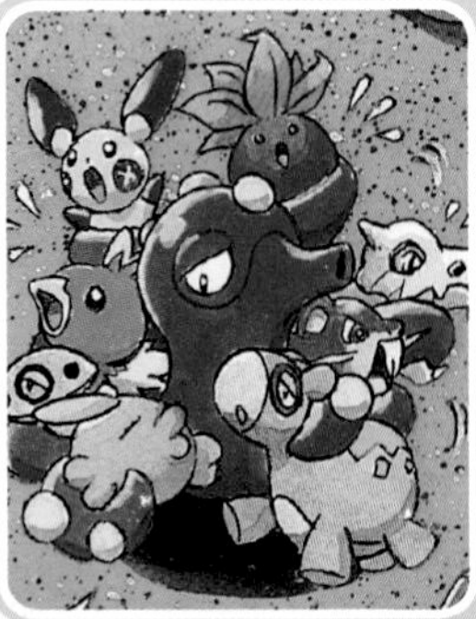

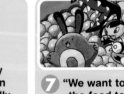

8 What's happening?

Octillery catches them one after another as if by magic!

Eight Pokémon are caught in all!!

9 There are 8 Pokémon and Octillery only has 8 arms. Hee hee hee, I can't get caught!

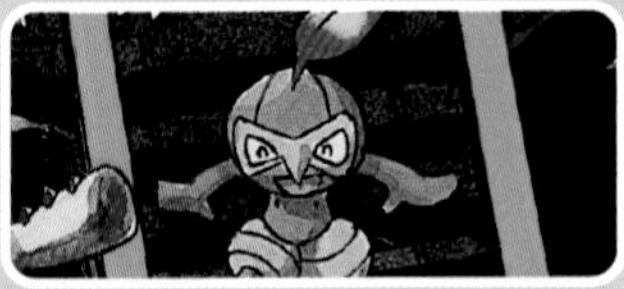

The feast is mine!!

10 Nuzleaf was too hopeful. It gets caught too.

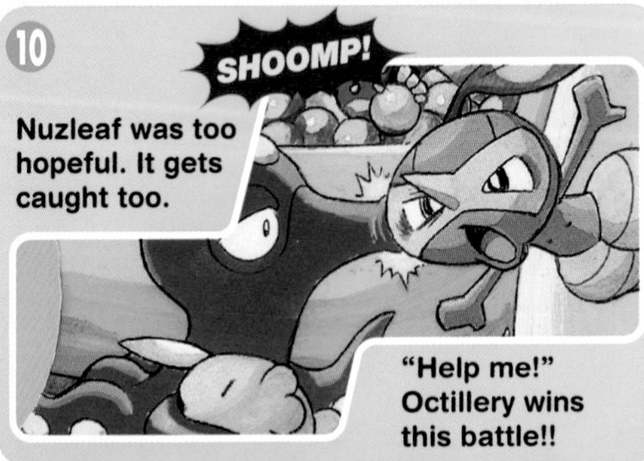
SHOOMP!

"Help me!" Octillery wins this battle!!

There are no actual answers for the Story Problems. If you read it in order, it becomes a story. See if you can find these scenes hidden in the puzzle pages!

Story Problem #3

Good Times at the Party

1 The party is beginning. The Pokémon are starting to gather.

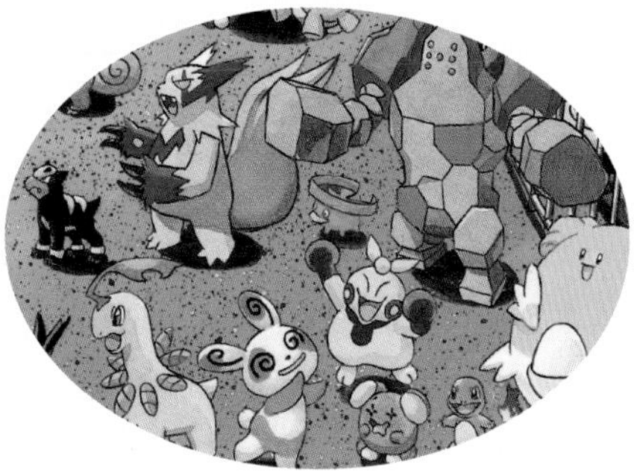

2 "Hello, it's been a while."

"How are you doing?"

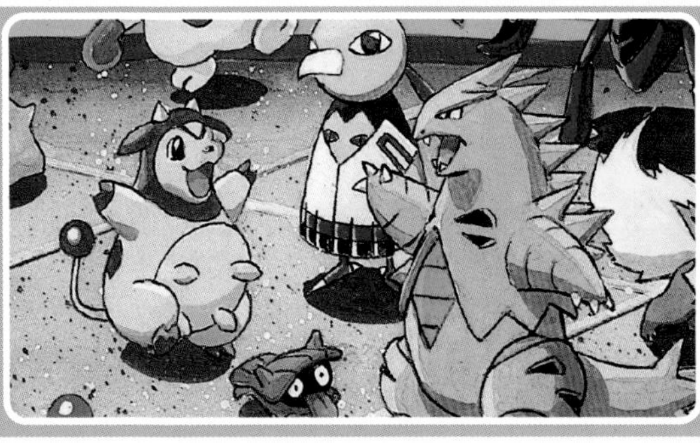

"How have you been lately?"

The conversations become lively amongst friends.

3 What a wonderful feeling.

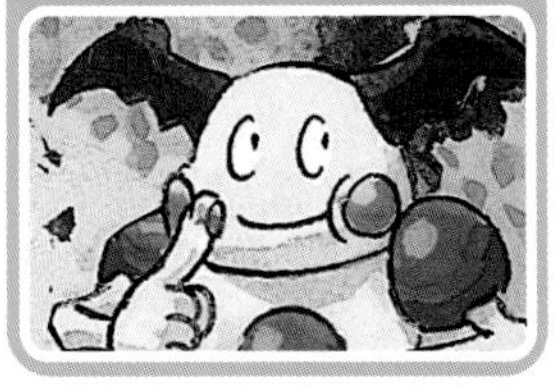

4 Mr. Mime is so excited and starts performing.

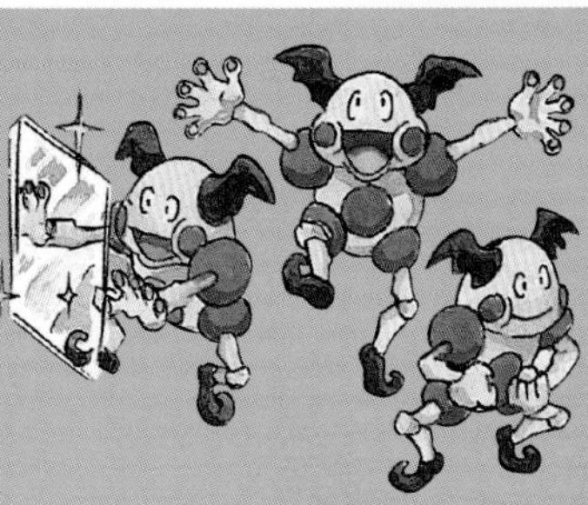

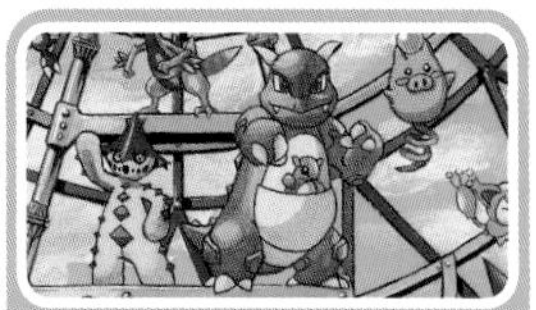

5 Then Kangaskhan shows off its favorite move, Dizzy Punch!

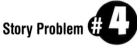

6 Camerupt livens it up by erupting!

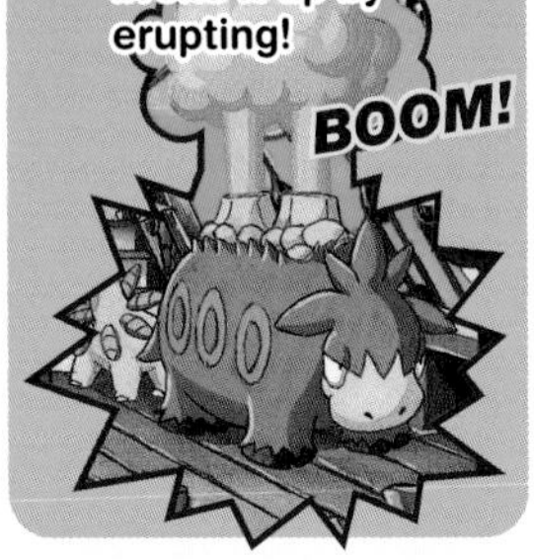
BOOM!

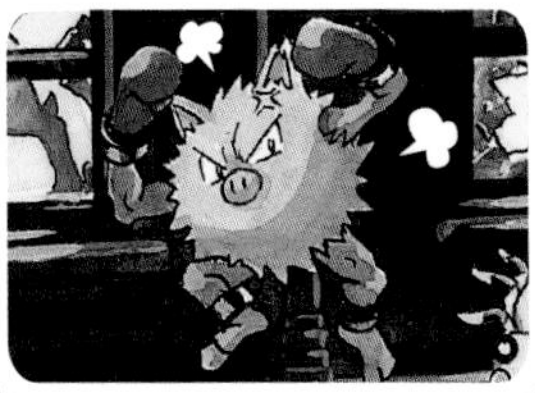

7 Primeape talks arrogantly, acts wildly... Oh, it's the same as always.

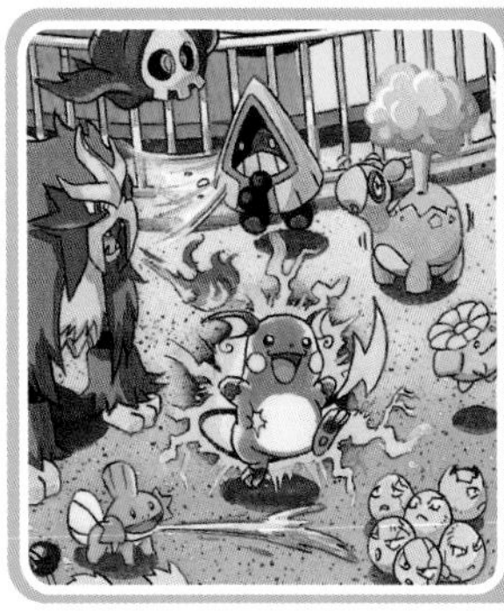

8 Oh no, everybody has started to do whatever they please! It's total chaos!

Story Problem #4

What's the Present?

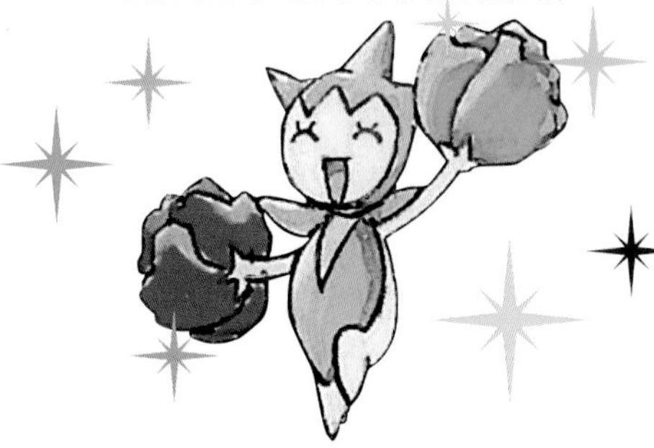

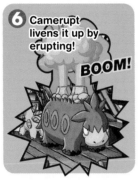

1 "Everybody, welcome to my birthday party today! ❤"

Roselia has appeared!

2 Happy birthday! This is a present from my heart.

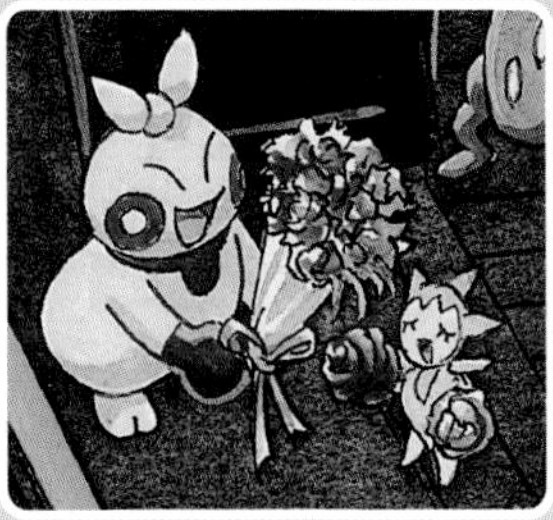

My, what lovely flowers!

3 I brought a cool present too. It's a headband to show fighting spirit!

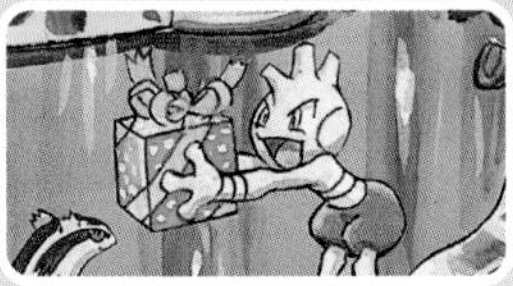

4 Hmm, it looks like it'll be useful in battle.

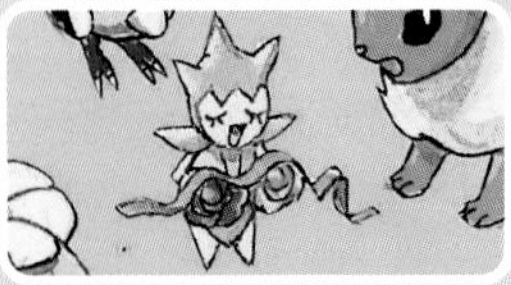

5 Oh Jigglypuff, what's the matter?

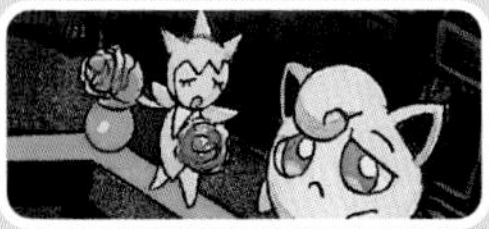

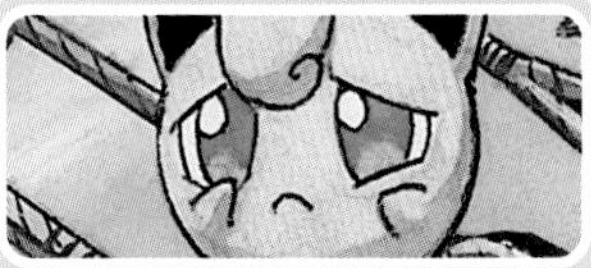

6 Jigglypuff...forgot to bring a present... That's why...

7 I'll sing a song! ❤

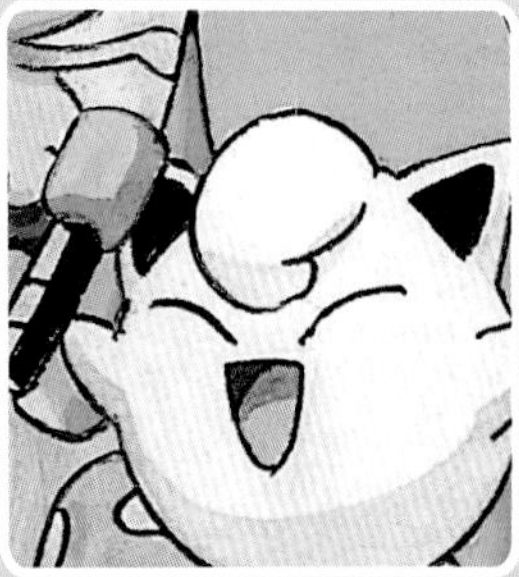

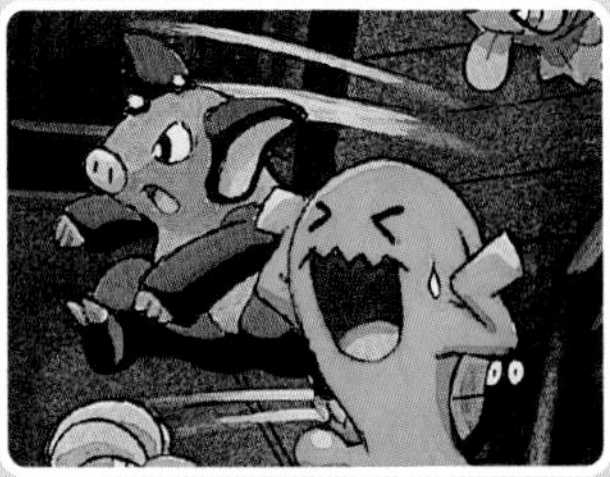

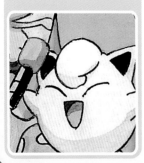

8 Aghh! Stop it, stop it! Somebody make it stop!!

9 ...It was too late.

While everybody sleeps peacefully, Jigglypuff starts a solo performance.

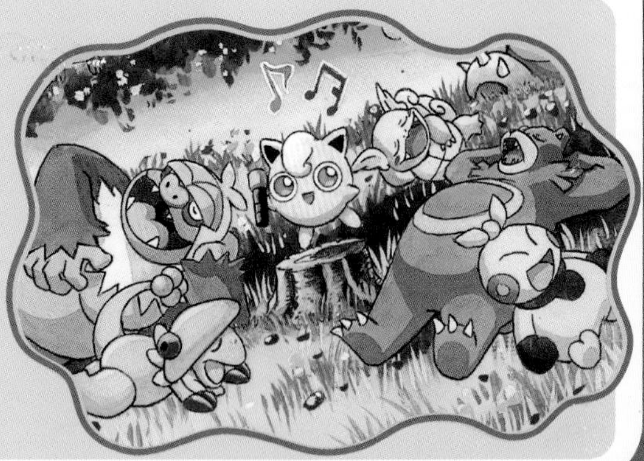

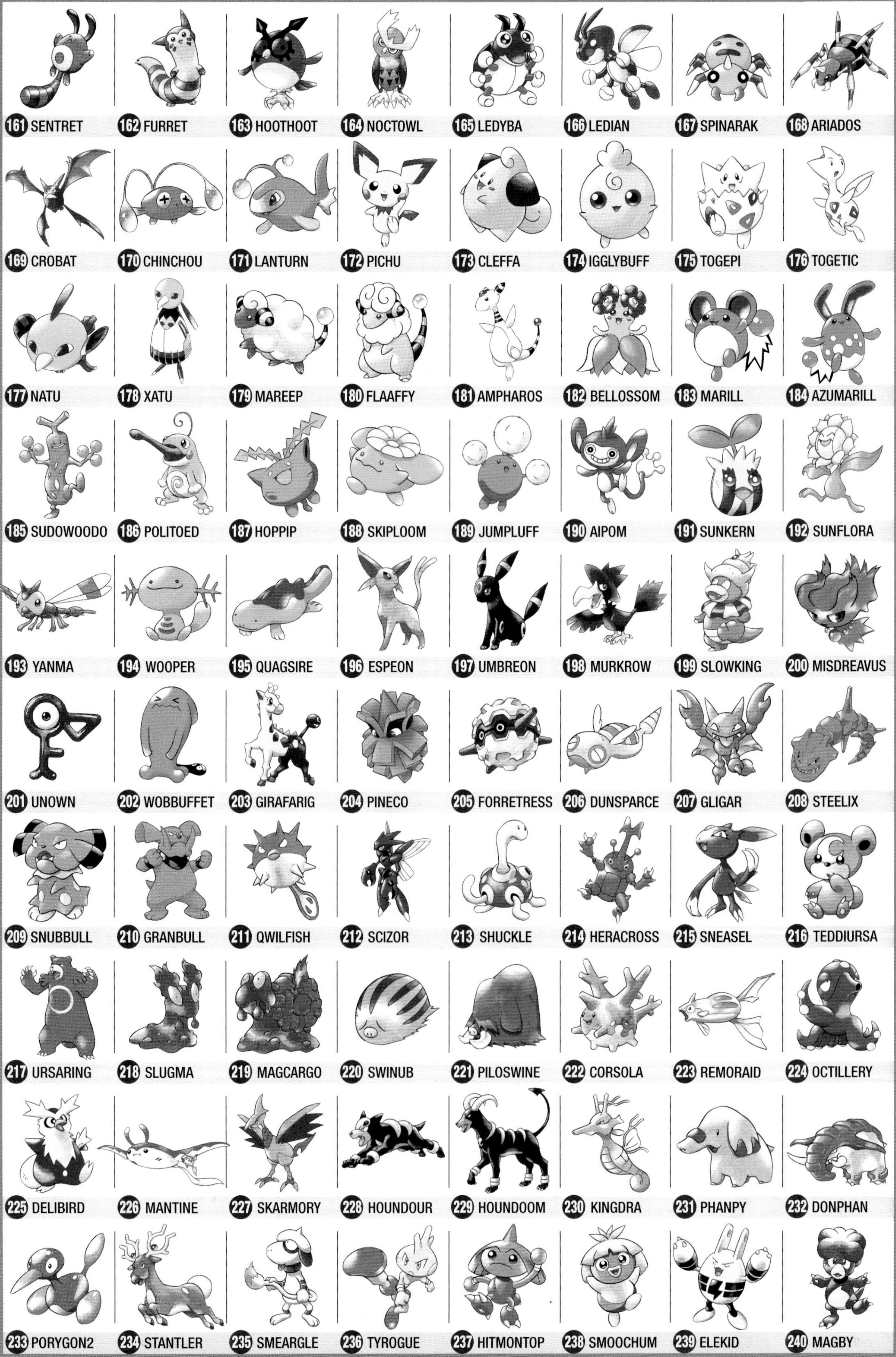
161 SENTRET
162 FURRET
163 HOOTHOOT
164 NOCTOWL
165 LEDYBA
166 LEDIAN
167 SPINARAK
168 ARIADOS
169 CROBAT
170 CHINCHOU
171 LANTURN
172 PICHU
173 CLEFFA
174 IGGLYBUFF
175 TOGEPI
176 TOGETIC
177 NATU
178 XATU
179 MAREEP
180 FLAAFFY
181 AMPHAROS
182 BELLOSSOM
183 MARILL
184 AZUMARILL
185 SUDOWOODO
186 POLITOED
187 HOPPIP
188 SKIPLOOM
189 JUMPLUFF
190 AIPOM
191 SUNKERN
192 SUNFLORA
193 YANMA
194 WOOPER
195 QUAGSIRE
196 ESPEON
197 UMBREON
198 MURKROW
199 SLOWKING
200 MISDREAVUS
201 UNOWN
202 WOBBUFFET
203 GIRAFARIG
204 PINECO
205 FORRETRESS
206 DUNSPARCE
207 GLIGAR
208 STEELIX
209 SNUBBULL
210 GRANBULL
211 QWILFISH
212 SCIZOR
213 SHUCKLE
214 HERACROSS
215 SNEASEL
216 TEDDIURSA
217 URSARING
218 SLUGMA
219 MAGCARGO
220 SWINUB
221 PILOSWINE
222 CORSOLA
223 REMORAID
224 OCTILLERY
225 DELIBIRD
226 MANTINE
227 SKARMORY
228 HOUNDOUR
229 HOUNDOOM
230 KINGDRA
231 PHANPY
232 DONPHAN
233 PORYGON2
234 STANTLER
235 SMEARGLE
236 TYROGUE
237 HITMONTOP
238 SMOOCHUM
239 ELEKID
240 MAGBY

Continued from page 3

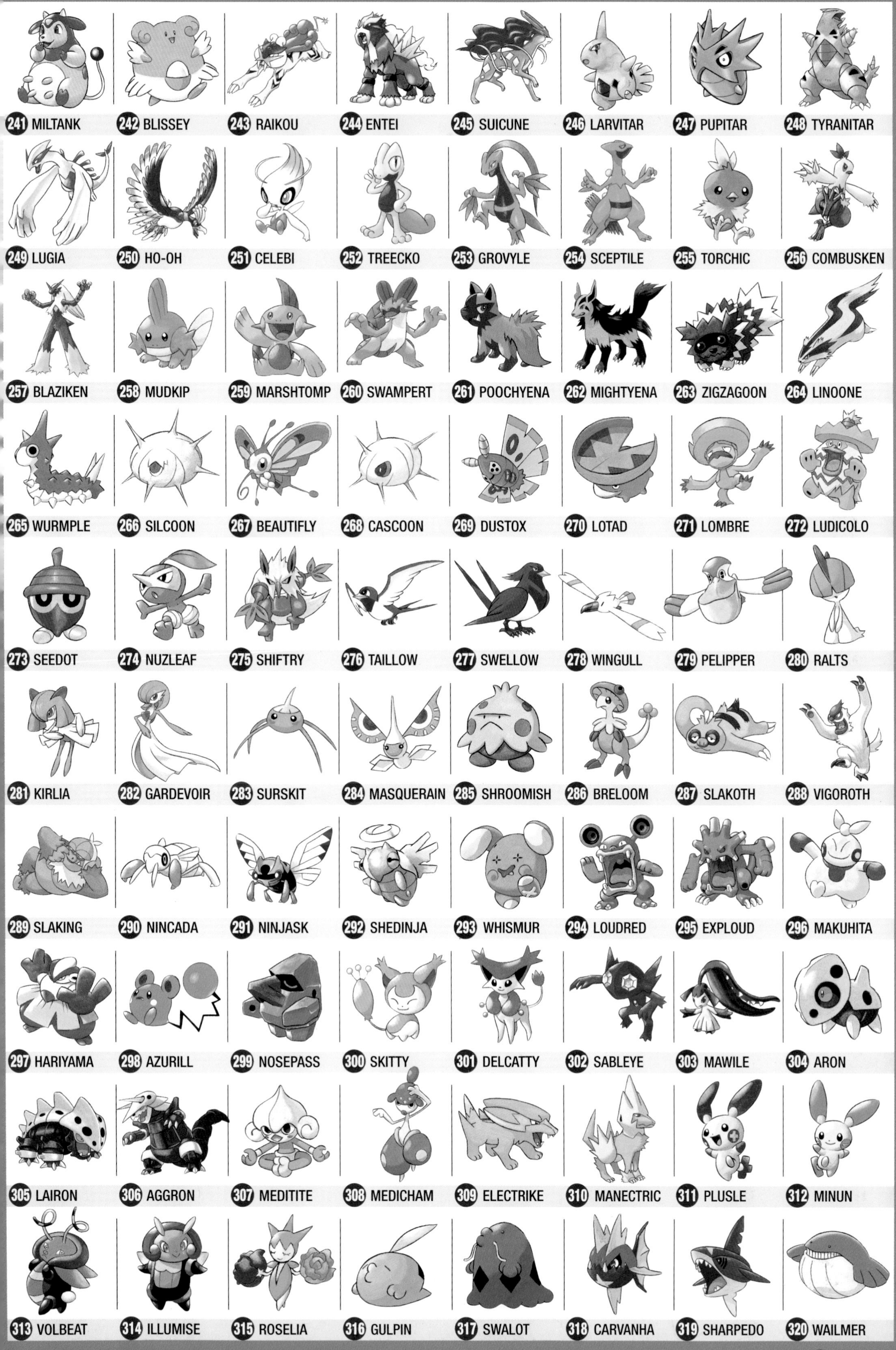
241 MILTANK
242 BLISSEY
243 RAIKOU
244 ENTEI
245 SUICUNE
246 LARVITAR
247 PUPITAR
248 TYRANITAR
249 LUGIA
250 HO-OH
251 CELEBI
252 TREECKO
253 GROVYLE
254 SCEPTILE
255 TORCHIC
256 COMBUSKEN
257 BLAZIKEN
258 MUDKIP
259 MARSHTOMP
260 SWAMPERT
261 POOCHYENA
262 MIGHTYENA
263 ZIGZAGOON
264 LINOONE
265 WURMPLE
266 SILCOON
267 BEAUTIFLY
268 CASCOON
269 DUSTOX
270 LOTAD
271 LOMBRE
272 LUDICOLO
273 SEEDOT
274 NUZLEAF
275 SHIFTRY
276 TAILLOW
277 SWELLOW
278 WINGULL
279 PELIPPER
280 RALTS
281 KIRLIA
282 GARDEVOIR
283 SURSKIT
284 MASQUERAIN
285 SHROOMISH
286 BRELOOM
287 SLAKOTH
288 VIGOROTH
289 SLAKING
290 NINCADA
291 NINJASK
292 SHEDINJA
293 WHISMUR
294 LOUDRED
295 EXPLOUD
296 MAKUHITA
297 HARIYAMA
298 AZURILL
299 NOSEPASS
300 SKITTY
301 DELCATTY
302 SABLEYE
303 MAWILE
304 ARON
305 LAIRON
306 AGGRON
307 MEDITITE
308 MEDICHAM
309 ELECTRIKE
310 MANECTRIC
311 PLUSLE
312 MINUN
313 VOLBEAT
314 ILLUMISE
315 ROSELIA
316 GULPIN
317 SWALOT
318 CARVANHA
319 SHARPEDO
320 WAILMER

Continued on the next page

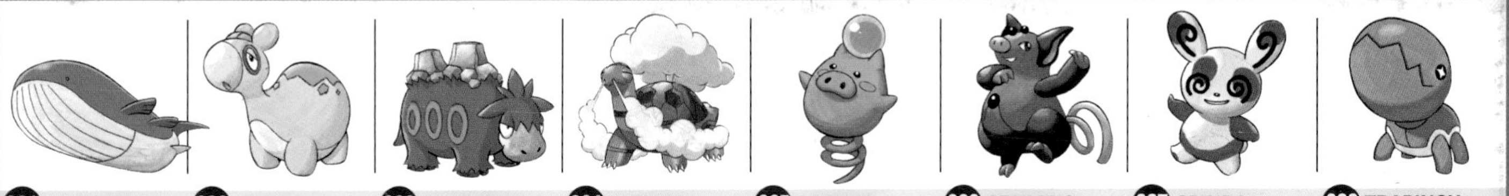

321 WAILORD | 322 NUMEL | 323 CAMERUPT | 324 TORKOAL | 325 SPOINK | 326 GRUMPIG | 327 SPINDA | 328 TRAPINCH

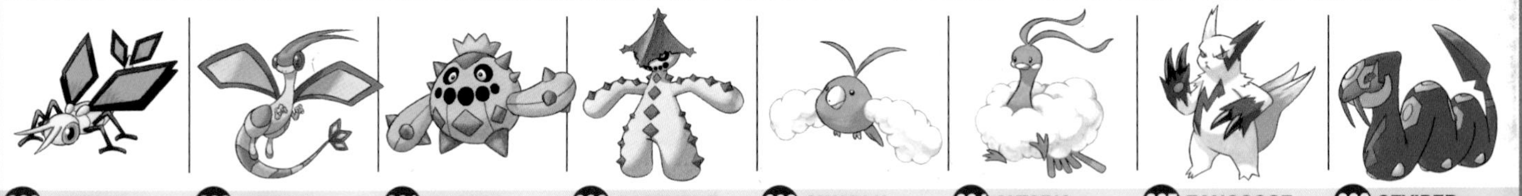

329 VIBRAVA | 330 FLYGON | 331 CACNEA | 332 CACTURNE | 333 SWABLU | 334 ALTARIA | 335 ZANGOOSE | 336 SEVIPER

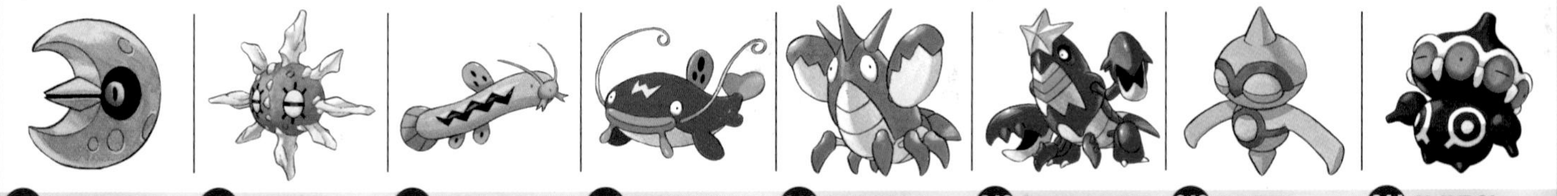

337 LUNATONE | 338 SOLROCK | 339 BARBOACH | 340 WHISCASH | 341 CORPHISH | 342 CRAWDAUNT | 343 BALTOY | 344 CLAYDOL

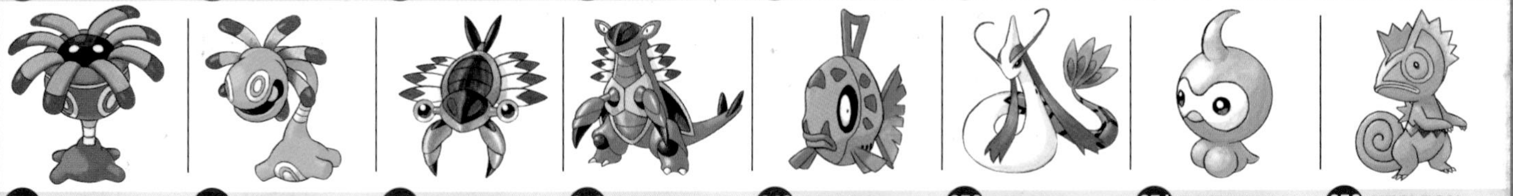

345 LILEEP | 346 CRADILY | 347 ANORITH | 348 ARMALDO | 349 FEEBAS | 350 MILOTIC | 351 CASTFORM | 352 KECLEON

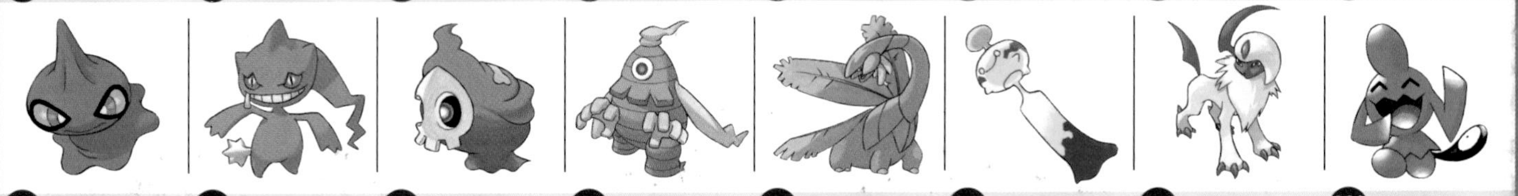

353 SHUPPET | 354 BANETTE | 355 DUSKULL | 356 DUSCLOPS | 357 TROPIUS | 358 CHIMECHO | 359 ABSOL | 360 WYNAUT

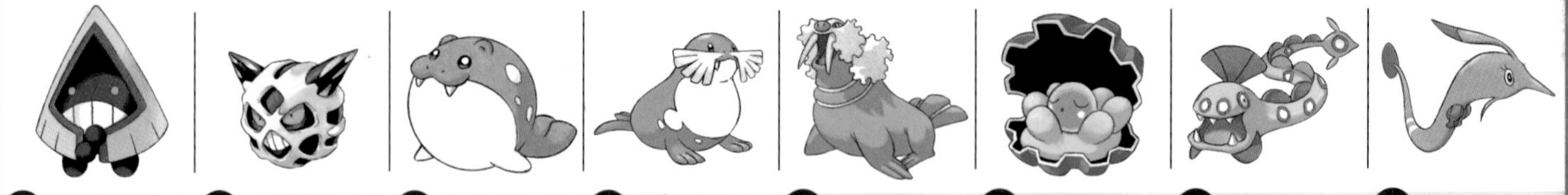

361 SNORUNT | 362 GLALIE | 363 SPHEAL | 364 SEALEO | 365 WALREIN | 366 CLAMPERL | 367 HUNTAIL | 368 GOREBYSS

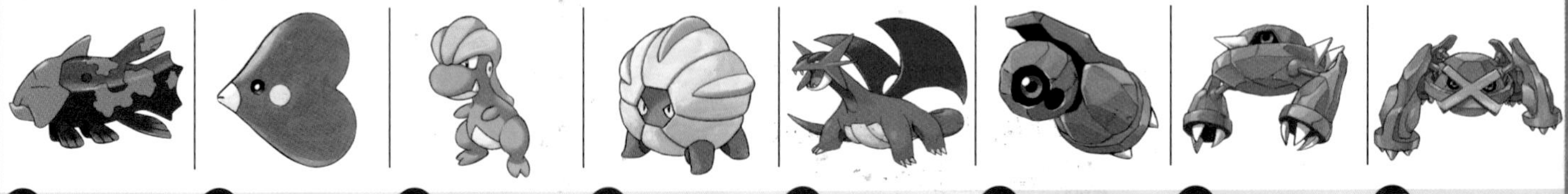

369 RELICANTH | 370 LUVDISC | 371 BAGON | 372 SHELGON | 373 SALAMENCE | 374 BELDUM | 375 METANG | 376 METAGROSS

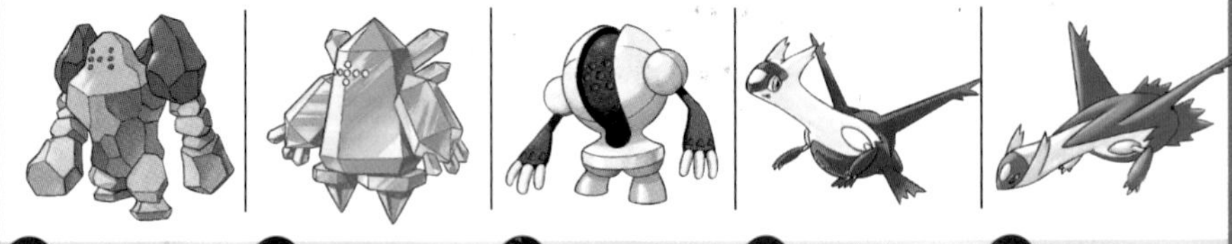

377 REGIROCK | 378 REGICE | 379 REGISTEEL | 380 LATIAS | 381 LATIOS

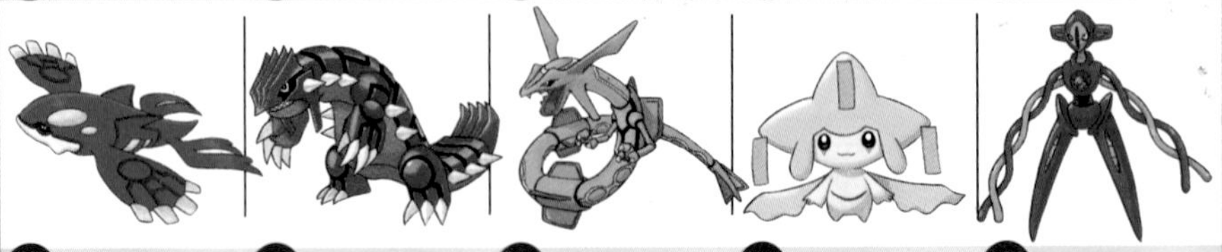

382 KYOGRE | 383 GROUDON | 384 RAYQUAZA | 385 JIRACHI | 386 DEOXYS

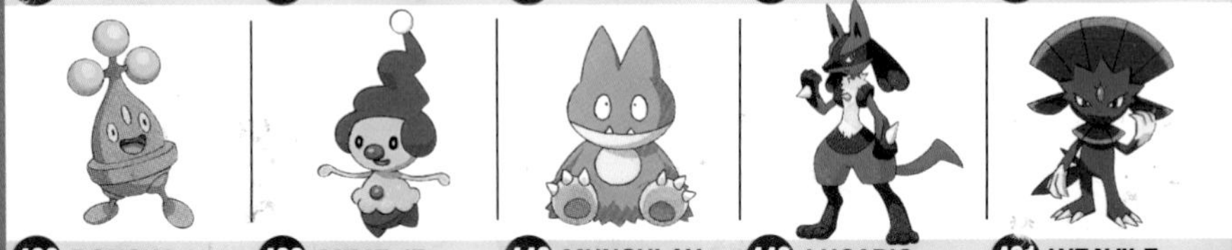

438 BONSLY | 439 MIME JR. | 446 MUNCHLAX | 448 LUCARIO | 461 WEAVILE

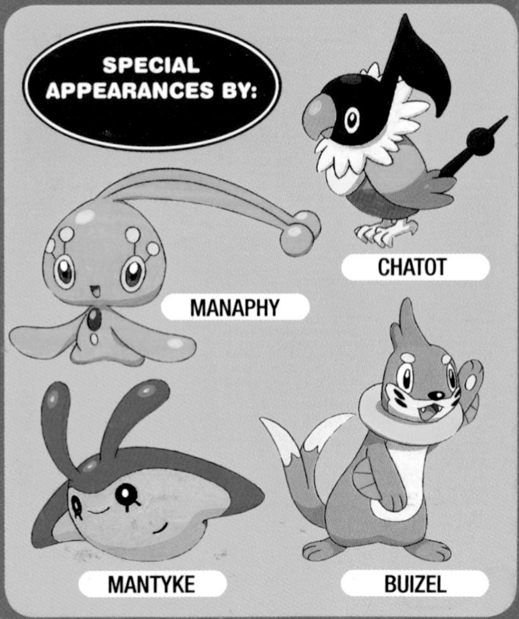
SPECIAL
APPEARANCES BY:
CHATOT
MANAPHY
MANTYKE
BUIZEL

Continued from the previous page